THE BOUND LEGACY

THE BOUND LEGACY

LEGACY OF THE SHADOW'S BLOOD™ BOOK 2

E.G. BATEMAN

MICHAEL ANDERLE

THE BOUND LEGACY TEAM

Thanks to our Beta Readers:

Erika Everest, Nicole Emens, Jim Caplan, Mary Morris, John Ashmore, Kelly O'Donnell, Larry Omans, Michael Baumann

Thanks to our JIT Team:

Dave Hicks
Deb Mader
Debi Sateren
Diane L. Smith
Dorothy Lloyd
Erika Everest
Jackey Hankard-Brodie
James Caplan
Jeff Eaton
Jeff Goode
John Ashmore
Lori Hendricks
Micky Cocker

Misty Roa
Paul Westman
Peter Manis
Rachel Beckford
Veronica Stephan-Miller

Editor
SkyHunter Editing Team

CHAPTER ONE

Amy lay motionless in the coffin and remained as quiet as she could. She was fairly sure the museum would be empty by now, but there was another reason to not move. The padding beneath her was hard and uncomfortable and every time she shifted even slightly, her nose was assaulted by a musty smell.

It had never occurred to her before that coffins didn't need to be as comfortable as they looked. The user wouldn't ever leave a one-star review on TripAdvisor. She might, though. *Museum of Death. One-night stay. Coffin extremely uncomfortable, no breakfast.* She stifled a giggle, then sighed. She wondered—and not for the first time—why on earth she'd said yes to this ridiculous plan.

As Jamal had explained it, she had to be the one to do it because the coffin was so stupidly small that only she would fit. She could have argued or flat-out refused. There were probably a few places he could have hidden. But, of course, she had relented. She always did with him. One look into those dark-brown eyes and her bones simply melted, along with any semblance of common sense.

She wondered what might happen if she were caught there. If she finally sat up to find herself surrounded by police officers.

She could be kicked out of medical school, for one thing. And what might possibly be worse, her parents would discover she wasn't spending summer break with Julie's family in the Hamptons. She was in fact, shacked up with her boyfriend in New Orleans. She had to stop herself from giggling again. Her dad would have a stroke.

Jamal had been desperate to come. He was obsessed with the place—and with voodoo—and told her he wanted to "find his people."

So much for that idea. She frowned in the darkness.

The locals treated him like a tourist wannabe and didn't understand how serious he was about it. If she was honest, she didn't get it herself. She didn't know whether she believed or not, but she didn't like to see her boyfriend dismissed so casually. They'd both eaten nothing but ramen and worked extra shifts for months to afford this break. But at the end of the day, their response didn't matter. This would show everyone.

He was about to get a top-level recommendation—one they couldn't ignore. *The* top-level, if what Jamal said was true.

A bead of sweat trickled down the side of her face and entered her ear. At least she hoped it was sweat.

Fuck this. I'm getting out.

She pushed the lid up and moved it to the side. When she sat, it slid off. Too slowly, she lurched out to catch it and missed. She hunched her shoulders and gritted her teeth as it fell to the floor with a bang. The sound was like an explosion in the stillness of the room.

If anyone was in the building, that noise would definitely bring them running. She waited.

After a few moments of silence, Amy drew the cellphone from her purse and clicked its flashlight on to find her bearings inside the Museum of Death. Carefully, she climbed from the coffin and dusted herself off with her hands. She played the light around the room and caught dust motes from the disturbed coffin in the beam.

Instruments of torture, autopsy photos, and newspaper headlines with pictures of serial killers were illuminated. As she flicked the light around, a death mask loomed out of the darkness. She stumbled back against the coffin. It wobbled on the stand and for a breath-holding moment, she thought it might collapse, but it settled. She blew stray bangs away from her face.

As a med student, she had seen corpses and witnessed a couple of autopsies. Death didn't frighten her, but still.

This place is creepy as hell.

She crept through the rooms and finally located a glass cabinet. A photograph above it was easily identifiable as the much-adored voodoo queen, Marie Laveau. With a slow and cautious motion, she stroked the face in the picture. In front of that and beneath the glass were several pieces of her jewelry. There were other trinkets and pictures, but they didn't interest her. She pulled at the frame, but nothing budged. Irritated, she cast the light over the cabinet and found a keyhole. It was locked.

"Shit!" She glanced around the room. Jamal was relying on her. She'd come this far and wouldn't go home empty-handed.

Amy approached a wall display and lifted a heavy metal surgical implement from its bracket. As a medical student, she should know what it was called. Jamal would know. She tested the weight in her hand and decided it would do.

Resolute, she returned to the cabinet, swung the instrument at the glass, and turned her face away at the last moment. She was rewarded by an almighty crash. Most of the top shelf disintegrated and the jewelry and pictures fell to the shelf below.

Hastily, she picked through the glass but withdrew her hand quickly. "Son of a bitch!" She had cut her fingers and looked at the incisions in the light from her cell. They were minor but stung a little, which merely increased her irritation. She played the light over the tiny shards again until she saw the glint from a ring. That was it. She was done. Without care for any further possible injury, she brushed the glass aside, snatched the ring, and ran to the door.

The apartment, fortunately, was only a couple of blocks away and a few minutes later, she burst through the door, closed it with her butt, and leaned against it. She had run all the way and heaved breaths with her hand on her chest.

Jamal walked through from the living room. "Did you get it?"

Instantly, she was annoyed. "Yes, Jamal, this *is* blood and it *does* hurt."

He walked to her and cupped her hand tenderly in his. His gaze settled on the ring which glinted in the light while a trail of blood dribbled into her palm from her fingers.

Amy looked at him and realized he wore only his shorts. The air-con was off and a sheen of sweat covered his body. White dots of paint trailed intricate swirling patterns around his face and chest, starkly vivid against his dark-brown skin.

"The blood will be good for the ritual." He plucked the ring from the little red puddle, turned away, and headed toward the living room.

She rolled her eyes, followed, and noted the flickering light from the many candles around the apartment. He'd already started the ritual.

Reverently, he placed the ring onto a bed of herbs and flowers in a wooden bowl and turned to her. His eyes flashed in the candlelight as he looked at her with hunger. It was almost her favorite part. This had all been totally worth it.

Jamal approached her with an intensity in his eyes that thrilled her. As he undressed her silently, her heart skipped a beat. He led her into a circle he'd marked out with chicken bones, picked up two cups, and passed one to her. She sniffed the contents. The drinks always smelled disgusting and they tasted worse, but they made her fly. She drank without hesitation.

He muttered words with a creole lilt to his voice that—being from Boston—he didn't usually have.

While she admitted to being somewhat naive regarding Jamal, she was generally cynical by nature and suspected this was all bullshit. That said, the sex was great. They'd complete his little ritual and get down to it.

Entirely focused, he dipped his fingers into a dish of oil fragranced with herbs and trailed them over her body while he muttered words she didn't understand.

Finally, he took the ring from the wooden bowl and indicated to her to kneel. Once he'd slid it on her finger, he cried, "I beg and implore to speak to the lady of New Orleans of old, the owner of this ring, and to see her made flesh again."

I hope she won't be disappointed to find herself in my skinny white body, Amy thought as she played along.

The drink began to take effect and she closed her eyes as she swished her long blonde hair around. She hoped they would get to the best part soon.

CHAPTER TWO

"You have to know where it is." Scott hovered in Lexi's peripheral vision, seated on his bed in their New Orleans hotel room.

Her eyes strained as she stared unblinkingly at a toothbrush, the subject of her latest lesson in magic. "I can see where it is. I'm looking directly at it."

"Not only with your eyes." His voice had taken on a Zen-like tone that made her want to smack him—or maybe worse.

"What else am I supposed to look with? My teeth?" She shifted her position on the end of her bed but kept her gaze on the toothbrush on the table.

"With every fiber of your being—you must know where the object is in the universe."

"I know where in the universe it will be." She pushed the words out and clamped her jaw again.

Scott cleared his throat. "Try not to have thoughts like that. If it ends up there, I will not be happy."

Despite the cool, air-conditioned room, prickles of sweat broke out on her forehead and neck. Her hand was clasped over the unhealing scar on her arm, the reservoir of magic she borrowed from him.

"Now, think about where you want the object to appear. Without looking at its destination, command it to be there."

Her gaze flicked involuntarily to the opposite side of the table, where the toothbrush was supposed to appear.

"Shit!" Lexi scowled as the magical connection was broken. The energy built up within the toothbrush careened it across the room and imbedded it in the wall. "There, I moved it."

"Hang on. I'll put it back and we can start again." Her friend climbed off his bed. He had almost taken hold of the toothbrush when he jumped away in alarm as it was joined in the wall by a knife. He gaped at her.

"If you take that toothbrush out of the wall, you won't wake up tomorrow morning." She bounced the tip of another blade against her fingers, ready to throw.

"Fine, it's your toothbrush." He rolled his eyes and returned to his bed to sit cross-legged. "Look, you always complain that your legacy abilities aren't as good as they should be. Building up your ability to use magic will help with that. If you're not strong enough to lift a car, you can lift it with magic. Not fast enough to save a life? Save them with magic."

She pulled her hair out of the ponytail and rubbed her scalp. "I don't understand why this is so hard. The other things I've tried to do with magic work fine."

"Some things are harder. Teleporting is hard but you'll get it. And you need to break the bad habit of touching the scar when you draw magic." He stretched his head to the side and cracked his neck.

Lexi looked at her unhealing scar. "I'm empty again. Why does it simply drain out of me like that? Even when I don't use it?"

"I don't know. But as long as we stick with each other, it'll never be a problem."

She leaned back on her bed. "Maybe *you* should spend time

training. You don't practice weapons training nearly enough, or hand-to-hand combat."

"So, you can get me in a headlock and give me a wet-willy again? I don't think so." Scott poked his nose.

"Are you picking your nose?" She screwed her face up in distaste.

"I'm not picking it. Magic tickles the hairs in my nostrils. It's so annoying." He moved to sit in front of the mirror and held his hand out, and a little pair of scissors appeared. With his nose raised, he gazed up his nostrils and went to work.

"Gross!" She threw a cushion at him. "There's a mirror in the bathroom for that."

A knock at the door drew their attention. He looked at Lexi, whose bed was closest to the door. She returned the look and didn't move. Finally, he rolled his eyes dramatically, flicked his hand, and the door opened.

"Hello, boys and girls. How are you settling in?" Dick entered with Marcel in his arms and waved the puppy's little paw at them. At the sight of the sorcerer in front of the mirror, he put the dog onto Lexi's bed, walked over, and sat beside him. "What are you watching—anything good?"

"Nothing. I'm trimming my nose hair." Scott waved the scissors.

"Scott!" Dick moved away from him. "Surely there's a mirror in the bathroom for that."

"Fine!" The young man stood and retreated to the bathroom.

Dick sat before the mirror and ran a finger along his eyebrow. "Wait, can you wind this back before you go?"

Scott turned with a look of disgust. "No. I won't invade someone's privacy for your entertainment."

"You did it before." The vampire sulked. He shifted his gaze to Lexi in the mirror and raised an eyebrow at her. She shrugged.

The request made her think about the woman who had died in their Palm Springs motel room before they had arrived. Her friend had insisted on using magic to reverse what the mirror had captured to watch the woman's tragic last minutes. She glanced at Scott. He didn't meet her gaze, though. She knew that empathy and emotion played a big part in sorcery and made for a controlled, compassionate mage.

Without the empathy, he'd be a monster like Caleb was.

She still wondered if he was too tenderhearted for the job.

"That was different." Scott turned away and managed two more steps.

Dick finally dragged himself away from his reflection. "How is it different?"

"It was my way of making her last moments... I don't know...not be alone." He shrugged, walked into the bathroom, and closed the door.

The vampire turned to her. "He's annoying and adorable, all at once—" He stopped speaking when he saw her hold her sharp little knife by the tip of the blade and tap Marcel gently on the nose with the handle.

Lexi said, "Bop," when she tapped the puppy's nose, then moved the handle out of the way when he tried to bite it. "What can I say? He's a genius wrapped in a Care Bear inside a sulky teenager."

"I heard that," the sorcerer shouted through the bathroom door.

She looked up and noticed Dick staring at her hand with a frown. A little confused, she glanced at the blade in her hand. "Oh! right." She pocketed the knife and stroked the dog's head.

The vampire stood. "Well, before you slice and dice my little companion, I have to take him out for his evening constitutional. And I'll visit some old friends—if I still have any here. This hotel simply won't do."

At his dismissive tone, she glanced around the luxurious room and wondered what was wrong with it.

Scott stuck his head out of the bathroom. "Are you kidding?

It's better than what we usually get by a mile. You've seen what we usually get. There's a gym downstairs and a pool on the roof. There are batteries in the TV remote, and it has air-con."

Dick flicked his hand toward him. "Oh! it'll do for you. I mean me—it won't do for me."

Lexi stopped rubbing Marcel's belly. "What's wrong with it—not enough designer furniture and half-naked young men, *Meester* Levine?"

He ignored her. "People in this town know me. I can't be seen in a hotel room with floor to ceiling windows. Exactly like I can't be seen drinking margaritas on Bourbon Street in the middle of the day."

She handed Marcel to him. "You can't spend all day hiding."

"I'll spend all day sleeping," he explained.

Scott returned to the room, "But you don't have to do that anymore." He stared from Dick to Marcel with a grin.

The vampire passed the puppy to him. "Have you ever switched shifts? It's like I've worked nights for over sixty years. It'll probably take me another sixty to get used to being awake during the day."

Lexi nodded. "The thought had never occurred to me. Although I'm surprised you don't own a place here already." She watched as he stepped to the mirror again.

He's probably checking that his face is still perfect.

"I did once, but Katrina had other ideas. I donated the land to the victims of the hurricane."

Scott put Marcel onto the floor and they watched as he padded to Dick, sat at his feet, and wagged his stumpy little tail from side to side.

He looked curiously at the vampire. "What will you do, then?"

"I have acquaintances who might be able to help. I think I'll—" He stopped speaking when he noticed the toothbrush and knife protruding from the wall. "Do you know—never mind." He shook his head. "I'll go see them now. Would you mind looking after Betsy? Maybe you could take her for something to eat? She's getting dressed." He turned to Scott. "Apparently, she's wearing a new dress. She's quite excited about it so be a decent chap and tell her she looks nice or something."

Dick opened the door and stepped into the hallway. He turned to them. "And please, make sure she doesn't get into trouble while I'm gone."

Lexi followed him to the door. "What trouble will a little old lady get into?" Dick was already heading down the hallway with Marcel doing tiny gallops next to him to keep up. She turned to Scott. "So basically, he's gone for a night out with his pals and saddled us with his eighty-year-old friend to look after. Why bring her if he intended to simply dump her on us? Dick is such a dick."

"I think it's sweet how protective he is of her." He checked the time. "It's been a long day of traveling. It's already ten pm and we don't want to tire her out. Maybe we could take her to the hotel restaurant for a little supper before bed." He retrieved his wallet from the dresser.

"Who's ready to hit the Quarter?"

The two friends looked toward the still open door and Betsy, who obviously wore her enchanted necklace. She looked like an eighteen-year-old and her dress was so short and tight that Scott's ears turned red. "You look nice," he said in a strangled tone.

Oh, dear!

"We're almost ready." Lexi's voice sounded a little strained, even to herself.

"Okay, I'll get my purse." Betsy beamed at them before she turned and headed to her room directly across the hall.

Lexi whirled to face her friend. "What have you done to her?"

"What? Why are you looking at me?" Scott shrugged as he put his wallet into his pocket.

She pointed across the hall. "She didn't look like that in Cabo."

"She wore that frumpy waitress dress in Cabo." He shrugged again. "This must be what she looked like when she was young."

"No one has ever looked like that. You have to fix it or we'll have to spend the whole night peeling douchey guys off her." She stormed past him and began to pick up various pointy objects and secrete them in the lining of her pants and vest.

The sorcerer shook his head vehemently. "I don't think she'll like that very much."

Lexi spun and punctuated her words with prods on his chest. "I don't think Mayor Todd will like that *you* made his mother look like a hooker."

"Come on. To be fair, that's the dress, not the necklace."

Betsy walked out of her room and across the hall into theirs. She sighed. "I think we might have a problem."

"Ya think? Sorry, I mean…what problem?" Lexi walked to the doorway and leaned against the open door.

"My ID says I'm eighty. Scott dear, could you rustle me up a new one?" She waved her fingers in pseudo magical waves in the air.

Scott looked at his partner.

She shook her head. "Sorry, Betsy, most of the bars in the French Quarter are run by supernaturals. A fake ID won't work on them." It wasn't true but the woman wouldn't know that. "How about Scott puts you safely into your fifties and you won't be asked?"

Betsy took a step back and covered the necklace with her hand. Her gaze slid to the side and Lexi was convinced she was about to bolt down the hallway in her five-inch heels.

Finally, the woman sighed. "Thirties. Not a day over thirty-two."

She nodded at Scott as Betsy headed into her room.

He muttered his incantation.

"Oh my!" Betsy said from across the hall a moment before she returned. Her body had lost its girlish frame and become curvier in very noticeable places. "Now you're talking. This dress will never do. I need to change."

Noticeably excited, she hurried to her room and closed the door.

The two friends stood side-by-side in the doorway of their room, their mouths in a perfect O.

Lexi recovered and punched Scott's arm before she scowled at the closed door. "You made it worse." When she received no answer, she glared at him. He blushed to the roots of his hair and she punched his arm again. "Try to remember she's old enough to be your grandma." She sighed. "This is all Dick's fault. I liked him more when I thought he was dead."

CHAPTER THREE

Dick sauntered through the Quarter with Marcel. They'd walked several blocks and the streets had quieted around them.

He stopped and took in the sight of the shadow of Jesus projected from the statue on to the back of St. Louis Cathedral. When he looked down, the puppy was doing his business.

"Marcel, really. In front of Jesus—have you no respect?" He pulled a little bag out of his pocket and cleaned it up.

"Good boy." He patted him on the head, tied the bag, and dropped it into a trash can.

That done, he turned his focus to a presence he'd been aware of for a few minutes. "You can come out, you know. I don't bite. Well, only recreationally."

A figure stepped from the shadows into the streetlight. "Hello, Mr. Levine. It's been a long time," said a deep creole voice.

The vampire studied the elderly African American man with grey dreadlocks who wore a monk-like cowl. He carried a staff with markings engraved on it and it was apparent that he leaned more heavily on it than he had in the past. "Hello, Joseph. It has. How are you?"

Joseph stopped at what was regarded in polite supernatural circles as a sensible distance away. "Happy and healthy and hoping to remain so."

Dick raised an eyebrow. "Then is it wise to wander alone at night?"

"I'm never alone. The spirits are always with me." The man spread his arms and a breeze swept through the street.

He sighed at the sudden cool breeze. "I don't imagine your spirits would consider following me around while I'm here?"

The man laughed. "You never did enjoy the climate of the Crescent City." His face lost its joviality. "So which faction have you come to join?"

"Faction? You're kidding me—that's still going on?" He shook his head, saddened by the revelation.

"Hostilities between the clans have simmered for years but it's blown up in the last few days. Things are changing in the shifter community too, although that's more civil. Everyone is restless. And here *you* are, coincidentally." He drew the last word out as though looking for the lie in it.

Dick tilted his head as he considered what he'd heard. "What do your spirits tell you?"

Joseph smiled. "They tell me you need another bag."

He looked down. "Marcel!" He slid his hand into his pocket again, thankful that he'd come prepared.

When he had tied the bag, the other man seemed to have made his mind up. "How about we get your dog a drink of water? He's safer off the street. We have rats bigger than him."

The vampire dropped the bag in the trash and lifted the puppy from the ground. "Don't you listen to him, Marcel. You are ferocious. I'll have you know Marcel recently saved me from a demented shifter." He stroked the animal's belly.

"Ah! A traitor to his kind." Joseph laughed.

They entered a tiny bar. From the outside, it looked like a house, but Dick had known of it for many years. He observed that it was full of humans. They stopped speaking and looked up when he entered.

"Let's go to the back." The other man led him through the building.

They entered a courtyard with greenery and flowers climbing the walls to the surrounding balconies and a trickling water-feature on the rear wall.

"This is charming." Dick took a seat in the little courtyard and sniffed the air. "Night-scented jasmine."

A woman came out and placed two whiskey glasses on the table and a water-filled bowl on the ground, which Marcel all but leapt into.

He scratched the puppy's head, then straightened to face his companion. "*Kouman timoun yo ye?*"

Joseph chuckled and he guessed his Creole was a little off. "The kids are well, thank you for asking. But not kids anymore and not interested in the old ways. Their gods are technology and money. So, if not to pledge allegiance to one of the clans, what brings you to town?" He leaned back and it was obvious that the man was more relaxed there. The vampire wondered what magic was in the walls to make him so confident but decided he didn't want to know.

"I'm visiting with a...for convenience, let's call her a friend. She's on a personal quest that has brought her to New Orleans and I offered to help." He tried not to stray anywhere in the discussion that would require him to lie.

"And your questing friend, where is she?" Joseph looked dramatically around the small courtyard as though someone might suddenly appear.

"Around. The hotel or a restaurant maybe. Detaching the fingers of a pickpocket is a distinct possibility. Who knows?"

Joseph leaned forward and shook his staff. "My spirits tell me something is different about you, William Levine."

Dick accepted the scrutiny for a few moments. Finally, he

lifted his glass. "A new conditioner. I'm worth it."

His companion laughed. They clinked glasses and drank.

Marcel went to Joseph and his stumpy tail wagged. He scratched the dog's neck, then produced a treat. Dick couldn't begin to guess where from.

The vampire nodded his appreciation of his drink before he returned to the subject at hand. "Who would you say is the more accommodating faction at the moment? I need a place to stay during the day."

"Ah yes, I remember your home. It was beautiful. It is an outreach center for the homeless now. Have you seen it?"

"I'm glad they were able to put it to good use, but no. I wouldn't like to see it so changed." For a moment, he looked into the middle distance and envisioned his New Orleans home of years gone by.

"I wouldn't suggest it's safe to go to any clan right now. Almost all of them demand that visitors show fealty. They all watch too much television. If the first one you visit can't help, you won't be welcomed by the rest. They won't talk to each other and they barely talk to me. Kindred is out of town and the clans talk about making grabs for power all over the place. You should go to the sanguinaires—the living blood drinkers. They're trying to stay out of this spat."

Dick was shocked. "Kindred is out of town? But why? I've never heard of such a thing. Are they on a team-building event?" He took a gulp of his whiskey. "Although it begs the question, how many Kindreds does it take to build a raft?"

"None," Joseph supplied. "They'd make us do it."

They laughed and clinked glasses again.

The man sniffed the air. "There is powerful, dark magic in the wind tonight, here and across the country."

Dick stroked an eyebrow absently. "Are the sanguinaires still at the same place?"

"Of course. Whether living or undead, we are all creatures of habit."

"I try not to be so predictable." He was a little offended.

"Do you still have that giant trunk you always travelled with? And the silver lion's head pin? You remain the only vampire I've ever heard of who wears silver."

"I stand corrected." He raised his eyebrows. "Apparently, I am predictable."

Joseph looked at Marcel. "Not completely. I must say, I never expected to see you with a puppy."

"He belonged to a friend who passed. We've found ourselves to be a surprisingly good fit." He leaned down, picked Marcel up, and stood. "Well, I'll say good evening, Joseph. Thank you for the drink and the information. Take care of yourself."

"I don't have to." The man smiled.

The vampire laughed. "Yes, of course. You have your spirits."

A breeze stirred the air in the courtyard and he breathed in the scent of the flowers. "Quite delightful." He nodded to Joseph and left.

The two continued through the streets until finally, Marcel refused to walk. He turned to the puppy who sat immovably and yawned. "Are you tired, little guy?" He picked him up and held him close to his face. "We're almost there." Marcel licked his nose.

Dick crossed the street and entered a bar. It had been a few years since he'd been there, but he recognized a few faces. They looked wary, though, which gave him pause.

A tall man stood. "Is that you, William?" He crossed to him and unsurprisingly, stopped a short distance away. The vampire stared at him in surprise. This convention wasn't usually followed by non-supernaturals, simply because there was no point. If any supernatural had ill-intentions toward this human, those few feet wouldn't save him.

"Hello, Oberon. I've heard things are tense these days and wonder if I could have chosen a better time to visit." He thought it best to clarify immediately that he wanted nothing to do with whatever the situation was between the clans.

His friend nodded at the message. "How can I help you?"

"I need a place to stay for a couple of nights. I'm with friends, but they can stay in a hotel."

"Martine?" Oberon called to a woman who stood behind the bar and she looked at him. "Is 3b in the apartment building free?"

She lifted a large black book and dropped it onto the bar with a thud before she pulled a pair of glasses from her head and propped them on her nose. Once she'd opened the book, she ran a finger down the page, then closed it. "It's free." She put the glasses onto her head again.

The man nodded, paused, then asked, "How about 3a, on the front?"

The woman stared directly at him in evident disapproval as she opened the book again and settled the glasses onto her face. She ran her finger down the page. "Yup." She made no effort to close it and simply stood and looked at him with exaggerated patience.

He stared in response.

Finally, she frowned. "What?"

Oberon put his hand out. "The keys?"

She rolled her eyes, lifted two keys from a shelf behind the bar, and handed them over.

The man looked at Marcel and grinned. "So, who's this? May I?" He held his hand still until Dick nodded. Cautiously, he put the back of his hand out for the puppy to sniff, then stroked the animal's head.

"This is Marcel. He's one of my traveling companions." He waved the tiny paw again and simply couldn't explain why it gave him such delight to do that.

Oberon looked at him, his expression somber. "Be careful walking the streets, my friend. Kindred is out of town."

He raised his eyebrows. "I heard. I've never known them to

leave New Orleans unprotected. I can't imagine what's holding it all together right now."

"It's only been a few days but it'll all hit the fan soon. We're simply trying to keep our heads down." The man shook his head.

Dick saw how worried he looked and knew he was right to be concerned. When things kicked off between supernaturals, it was often the humans who were caught in the middle. "Do you know why Kindred left? Where they've gone?"

"Apparently, some idiot opened a portal to a hell dimension in Palm Springs. Creatures have poured through for days—hundreds of them. Nasty buggers, it would seem."

"Oh, that. Yes, I'm aware." He wasn't quite sure what else to say.

Oberon's eyes narrowed. "Now that I think about it, isn't Palm Springs your neck of the woods?"

The vampire smiled. "And now you know why Marcel and I have chosen to put a healthy distance between us and home."

"It's perfectly understandable." The man handed the keys over.

Dick reached for his wallet. "How much do I owe you?"

"William, you insult me." Oberon put a hand up.

Martine picked a pen up. "Obe, what do I put in the book?"

The man looked at the vampire with his eyebrows raised.

"Dick."

The woman smirked. "Okay, and the other room?"

Oberon replied this time. "Marcel."

She wrote the names and snapped the book closed.

"Do you have time for a drink?" he asked.

"I need to get Marcel to his basket. Would you like to meet for dinner tomorrow evening?"

"I'd love to, William. But a couple of the clans—at least those who can stand to be in the same room—are meeting for a parlay tomorrow night. They've chosen my establishment to host it."

"What an honor," Dick said with an eyebrow raised to emphasize the sarcasm.

"Quite. It'll come to nothing, though. They'll bluster for a couple of hours, drink my best whiskey, and leave disgruntled." Oberon rolled his eyes. "Can I send a snack round?" He indicated two young women who donated blood to sanguinaires in the corner of the room.

"In public?" He raised a brow. Of course, he'd already been aware of the tang of blood in the air.

His friend laughed. "We're human, my friend. Kindred leaves us alone."

"Ahh. And no thank you. I'm fine. I dined early." He had brought a few blood bags in his temperature-controlled box as he preferred to be personally acquainted with the source. For now, he didn't want to risk it. The young ladies were probably in good health but one of the thugs who shot up his car in Palm Springs had given him an upset stomach for a couple of days. It wasn't worth the risk.

Outside the bar, Dick checked his cell and was rewarded with the location of the oyster bar where Lexi, Scott, and Betsy were. He attempted to put Marcel down to walk but the puppy would have none of it. With a chuckle, he conceded defeat and held the dog in his arms as he made his way through the streets.

CHAPTER FOUR

Lexi sat with Scott and Betsy in the small oyster bar on Bourbon Street.

She glanced yet again at the other woman's plunging neckline. "Where did you get those dresses?"

"I've been shopping on the Internet since Cabo. Everything was waiting when I arrived in the room." Betsy looked at herself. "Although I'll have to visit the stores tomorrow. This dress is a tight squeeze."

"I noticed." She raised an eyebrow.

The older woman's gaze slid over her leathers. "How can you bear to wear all that hide? You must be melting."

She sighed. In all honesty, she didn't have an answer and she *was* melting. New Orleans was so much worse than Palm Springs had been. She gazed around the room, noted that there didn't seem to be any supernaturals in sight, and decided to risk removing her jacket. "Is there anything you'd like to do while you're here, Betsy?"

"I'm not sure. I've only been to New Orleans once, with Harv. We didn't even visit the French Quarter. I stayed around the pool at the hotel for two days while he was at a conference, then we left."

Scott sat up excitedly. "You'll want to have a good look around while you're here then. Maybe we could take a tour."

The waiter appeared at the table and took their orders.

After he left, Betsy tutted. "Oh dear! I forgot to order one of those Hurricane cocktails everyone's drinking."

"I'll get it." Lexi stood and headed to the bar. She waited patiently at the busy counter for the drink and noticed that it became steadily louder thanks to a group of young men somewhere behind her. Finally, she took the drink, turned, and as she stepped away from the bar, bumped into someone.

A young man shook about a teaspoon of beer dramatically from his hand. "Hey—careful, stupid." His friends went silent.

He looked at Lexi. "Oh, sorry. I mean, my fault." At that moment, he looked like he might pee his pants.

Shit!

She didn't respond but returned to the table as the group shuffled into the back of the bar.

Back at the table, she stood for a moment, perplexed by the two hurricane cocktails already in front of Betsy on the table.

"Oh, some kind young men at that table over there heard me mention the drink and dashed to the bar." The woman gave a little finger wave to a group of three men at a nearby table who stared at her. Their thoughts were etched on their faces and it wasn't a pretty sight.

Lexi raised an eyebrow. "Well, that's not creepy."

Scott peered into the throng of people. "What's wrong? I felt you getting irate."

She signaled to him with a little twirl of her finger and he mirrored the motion as he muttered an incantation. He nodded that it was safe to speak.

"A few shifters saw my scar," she said as she pulled her jacket on again and sat. "I should have been more careful. All they have to do is mention me to local Kindred and we're in trouble."

"We won't be here long. Don't worry about it." Scott pulled the drink she brought closer to him. "I might as well have this. Betsy will be on the floor if she has all three."

Lexi smiled. "Sure."

The sorcerer looked like all his Christmases had come at once. He picked the drink up and turned to watch the people.

While he was distracted, she slipped her thumb up her sleeve and stroked the scar to activate its power. "I think these two should stay sober tonight," she whispered.

Scott turned to her, having felt the discharge of magic. "What did—"

"Excuse me."

She looked up in response to the nervous voice. It was the shifter again and he held another hurricane. "I'm sorry about that. I wasn't sure if I'd spilled your drink too so I got you another one." He held it out to her but she didn't take it.

This guy's so nervous, he's making me nervous.

"It's okay. It was my fault."

"I thought you were all away, clearing a mess up in Palm Springs." He left it hanging as though she might respond.

She didn't and he looked even more anxious.

"Well, here you go, anyway." He put the drink onto the table and stepped back.

"Thanks for the drink," she replied dismissively.

When he'd moved away, Scott took his cellphone out.

"Are you messaging Dolores?" Lexi asked and he nodded. She took a sip of her drink, screwed her face up, and pushed it away. "That's strong."

"Do you think so? It seemed strong at first but it tastes like fruit juice now." Betsy stirred her drink with the straw.

The sorcerer's gaze slid to Lexi and he gave her a look of pure disappointment.

She focused on the shifters, who filed out of the bar with their heads low.

Betsy shook her head. "Lexi dear, you killed their buzz."

"I didn't mean to. But it explains why they were being so raucous. They thought there were no Kindred in town to keep an eye on them."

Scott's phone beeped, and he picked it up to read the screen. "Dolores got out before Kindred arrived. No one will remember us except Edward, and he's out of Palm Springs too." He continued to read. "Well, that's interesting. No one remembers Caleb either."

A dark look crossed Betsy's face. Caleb had posed as a family friend and her husband's business partner for years before he murdered her husband, then brainwashed and almost murdered her son. "He was a prominent member of Palm Springs society. How could everyone forget him? I know I never will."

The sorcerer patted her hand. "They'll remember there was someone but not the details. Dolores says she wasn't responsible for that. It must have been part of how he manipulated everyone's minds."

The woman shook her head. "It seems impossible. He was a business owner. Who did all those people think they were employed by?"

"I have no idea. I'll ask Dolores next time we speak." He shrugged.

She looked at her cocktail and put her glass down, looking guilty. "Does she have any news about Todd?"

Scott smiled. "Yes. He's getting there. The scars have all healed but they're keeping him asleep while they repair his mind."

Lexi brushed her scar discreetly. *Okay, she can get a little buzzed.*

The food came and they talked casually.

Betsy finished her drink and banged her palms on the table.

"Wow! That drink really hit me. Let's dance." She stood and whirled into Dick.

"William!" She slapped her hands onto his cheeks and planted a kiss on his lips before she hugged him. "You've always been my favorite homosexual."

"Well, thank you. You're too kind." He examined her curiously. "Why Betsy, you've...grown." He smiled and gave her another hug. Then, over her shoulder, he mouthed, "what have you done?" to the two young people.

Lexi shrugged. Regulating someone's level of intoxication was harder than she thought, but she wasn't sure that was what Dick was referring to.

Betsy stepped back and patted his face again. "Dick, I'm going to the powder room. Oh...do you mind if I call you Dick?"

He shrugged and raised his palms. "Everyone else does."

"Dick, you must try the hurricane. It sneaks up on you and hits you between the eyes like a force-five." She tottered to the back of the room in her tight black satin dress.

Lexi noted that the three men who had bought her the drinks watched her progress.

The vampire shook his head and sat. "Harv would be spinning in his grave."

Scott put his arms out to Marcel and the other man passed him over for a little attention.

She turned to her friend and asked innocently, "Can you do anything to make her less drunk?"

He stared at her with his eyebrows almost at his hairline. "Gosh, what a good idea."

Before she could retort, he closed his eyes and muttered inaudibly.

"So..." Dick leaned forward. "I've got us a couple of apartments in the Quarter. We can move there tonight. And you won't believe what else I've heard—"

"That Kindred's moved en masse to Palm Springs?" Lexi winked at him.

"Oh, you know." He looked crestfallen. "How did you know?"

"I was careless and was seen by a pack of shifters. They saw the scar."

Scott finished his drink with a slurp of the straw. "I thought we'd taken care of everything in Palm Springs."

"Not quite," the vampire explained. "Those lower-level demons were still coming through a portal we didn't know about. Apparently, there are hundreds of them."

"Oops!" The younger man shrugged. "My bad."

Dick narrowed his eyes at Lexi. "What are you looking at?" He turned in his seat.

She nodded toward a table near them. "That table of three guys is now only two guys. I'm going to check on Betsy."

Before she could take a step toward the bathroom, Betsy came through the crowd with a dazzling smile. "I'm ready to go when you are."

They moved together to leave the restaurant. At the door, Lexi turned and as the crowd parted, saw the third creepy guy on the floor near the restroom, cupping his balls. She smiled.

On the street, she took the older woman's arm. "Have I told you that you are an absolute joy to be around?"

"Why Lexi, how sweet of you to say that." Betsy looked puzzled for a moment. "Where are we going now?"

"Dick has found somewhere else to stay. We have a place too if we want it. We're going to have a look," Scott explained.

As they wandered along Bourbon Street past the revelers, Lexi realized that she received a few strange stares. Not only that, people crossed the street to avoid her.

Dick had noticed it too. "Shifters are worse gossips than old ladies."

"Hey." Betsy tottered closer and thumped his bicep.

He took her arm. "I'm sorry, but I don't think a jury of your peers would find you guilty of being over twenty-five."

She smiled and raised her chin. "I'm thirty-two today."

"Hmm." He studied her for a moment. "You looked less trouble when you were eighteen."

The woman giggled.

They turned a couple of corners and stopped halfway down the street at a door beneath a gallery covered with baskets of flowers.

"This is delightful."

Lexi smiled. Betsy looked young but spoke like she was from another time, which of course, she was.

"I bet there's no gym or rooftop pool," Scott muttered.

They made their way to the third floor where the two apartments were located.

Dick produced a key and handed it to Scott. "Here's yours." He dangled another in the air. "And here's ours, Betsy dear. You'll have your own room and I'll feel better knowing where you are."

"Come on then, jailer, let me in." The woman smirked and rolled her eyes.

As always, Lexi walked into their apartment first. It was surprisingly modern, decorated in subtle grays with polished hardwood floors and modern furnishings. The only indication that the building was old was the high ceiling. The air-conditioning, along with ceiling fans, made the air crisp and cool, and she sighed.

She made her usual check of the rooms and ended in the bedrooms. One had a king-sized bed and the other held two queens. Even with two bedrooms, she knew they would bunk in one room. Some Kindred habits never left. Both rooms had floor-to-ceiling windows and doors onto the balcony at the front of the building.

Satisfied, she wandered across the hallway and into the other apartment. Being on the back of the building and closed in on both sides, it had no windows. It was perfect for a vampire.

Scott appeared in the doorway. "Do you want me to scoot back for the bags?"

Betsy shook her head. "Not for me. I'll need to pack. I'm afraid I went through the new clothes like a Tasmanian devil and they're everywhere." She headed into Lexi and Scott's apartment to have a look at it.

"I can bear witness to the fact that they are indeed everywhere." Dick rolled his eyes. "I haven't even opened the trunk yet—"

"Say no more." Scott disappeared.

Lexi returned to their apartment and stood at the doors to the balcony.

Betsy came in behind her. "What a lovely balcony." She stood beside her and stared out. "What will you do while I play the tourist?"

She retrieved the photograph she carried and stared at her young face smiling at her. "First, I'll go to where this was taken to see if it rings any bells. I'm not hopeful, though, and I suspect this memory is lost with a thousand others, wiped by Kindred." She returned the photograph to her pocket. "Then, I'll see a local witch, someone Dolores knows. She'll give me access to records about Kindred activity here about ten years ago. We might be able to trace the man in the picture."

Scott reappeared with Dick's trunk. He set it down, vanished again, and returned two minutes later with his and Lexi's bags. With a small smile, he passed the toothbrush and knife to Lexi. "I repaired the wall. The toothbrush was really embedded."

Her face colored. "Let's head to the hotel. Betsy can gather her gear and we can check out properly." The four of them locked the apartments and wandered downstairs.

Once on the street, they began to walk in the direction of Bourbon Street and their hotel beyond it. A clatter of footsteps made them all turn. A girl of about eleven or twelve years old ran toward Lexi. "You're needed," the youngster said, a little out of breath. "I been looking for you all over."

"Excuse me?" She was perplexed.

"There's been a robbery. They said to come get you." The girl was insistent and Lexi could sense that she was a shifter, although she was probably too young to have shifted yet.

Betsy glanced up and down the street. "Honey, maybe you should call the police. Don't you have an adult with you?"

"It's a community problem. I was told to come get *you*." The girl attempted to pull her now, her expression urgent.

Dick frowned at her. "Isn't this something your pack can deal with?"

"She's supposed to come. It's her job," the girl hollered and the words seemed to echo in the street.

Lexi looked up quickly and confirmed that a few people had stopped to watch them. Her gaze scanned the buildings, where people watched from windows.

"Fine, I'll come." She turned to Dick and Betsy. "Would you mind dropping our key card at the front desk?" She slid it from her pocket and passed it to him.

The two friends followed the messenger. Within a few minutes, she'd led them to the corner of a street and pointed to a store where a small crowd had gathered. "Over there." She ran quickly down the street before they could ask any other questions.

They stopped on the corner to speak, still a short distance away from the crowd.

"What do you want to do?" Scott asked. "We could simply leave town."

"What I want to do is run in the opposite direction like she did." Lexi pointed at the girl who'd already covered considerable ground. She sighed and thought for a moment. "With Kindred out of town, we won't have a better chance to follow up on the photograph, though. Okay, they think we're Kindred so let's be Kindred until we can get out of this."

They crossed the street and approached the store. She noted its name with a small frown. The Museum of Death wasn't what she'd have chosen for a tourist outlet, but maybe her experiences left her a little cynical.

She studied the crowd and briefly caught the gaze of an old man with dreadlocks who wore a monk-like cowl and carried what looked like a wizard's staff. He narrowed his eyes as he returned her gaze, then nodded once.

Weird.

A man stood in the doorway with keys in his hand and she focused on him. "So, what happened?"

He raked his fingers through his hair. "We think there's been a robbery."

"You think?" Lexi glanced at the small crowd and confirmed that the guy with the staff had disappeared as she'd suspected he would.

The key-holder continued. "The alarm on the front door tripped. When I got here, the door was unlocked—apparently from the inside—and a glass display case inside was shattered. We're not sure if anything has been taken as the manager's on vacation. I've looked after the place but I don't know the exhibit well. I can't tell what, if anything, is gone. I was told if anything happened to not call the police but to contact the owner's friend, Alice."

A woman stepped forward, who she guessed was Alice. "I tried calling but no one picked up. In the end, I had to send the kid out." Okay, so she wasn't Alice and was most likely the mother of the young girl.

"No worries. Let's see what we have." Lexi entered the museum and turned to find Scott still standing outside. He looked like he was working himself up to enter the building. Even with her stunted legacy abilities, Lexi could feel the presence of something within and already knew he wouldn't like it at all.

Once inside, he looked around and his face darkened.

They followed the man through a curtain to a back room.

He pointed at the coffin on a stand. "This isn't usually open. I think someone sneaked into it and climbed out after we'd closed for the night."

"Are you sure it wasn't only a prank? Maybe you should have simply called the cops." She looked at a shelf that held things in jars she'd rather not have seen.

The sorcerer gazed around. "There are...things in here. Things that aren't safe to be removed."

'That's why we called you," the man agreed.

Lexi looked at a row of death masks on the wall and scratched her scar absently.

This place is as creepy as hell.

Their guide pointed to a pile of broken glass in a cabinet with a few objects protruding from it. "This is the case they broke."

She looked at the glass. "I see that. Is everything usually left in darkness at night?"

"Back here is, yes."

"And no CCTV?"

"It's being upgraded. We're kind of between systems." He shrugged apologetically.

"Okay, leave us to work." She was keen to get out of this little shop of horrors.

The man walked through the curtain without protest and left them alone.

Scott gazed around. "I can't see the reflective surfaces being of much help if it was dark." He stood in the center of the room, faced the casket, and closed his eyes. She stood out of the way as he moved his hands in circles.

A shift in the air gathered a swirl of dust before it coalesced into the shape of a young woman with long hair seated in the casket. She dropped nimbly to the floor and looked around before she approached the case. Her hand rested on a photograph at the back of it for a moment before she retrieved some kind of implement, which she used to shatter the glass. She reached down, jerked back and appeared to look at her hand, then picked something up and ran out of the room.

Lexi walked to the picture. It was the only thing still upright above the mess of glass and artifacts.

"Hi," she shouted.

The man pushed through the curtain.

She tapped the woman's face. "This picture—who is it?"

He gaped at her. "Are you kidding?"

"Listen, I've had a long day and night."

"It's Marie Laveau. The Voodoo Queen."

"Oh right, of course." Even she had heard of her. "And what was directly in front of the picture?"

The man stared at the mess. "I think it was her ring."

"Okay. Don't touch anything with your hands." She removed a sharp-tipped knife from her pocket and handed it to him. "See if it's missing."

His expression a little anxious, he stooped and poked through the glass with the blade. "There's blood here."

Scott's eyebrows raised and his mouth opened, but she shook her head discreetly.

After a few moments, the man stood and handed the knife to her. "Yes, there's a ring missing."

Lexi slid it into her pocket. "It looks like a small, slim girl hid in the coffin, broke the cabinet and took the ring, and ran. See if any staff members can remember someone fitting that description entering the museum today. In the meantime, we're done here for now."

They walked out and headed toward the apartment.

"What do you think?" Scott asked as they walked.

"I think the real Kindred can deal with it when they get back. We have our own stuff to do."

He nodded. "Is that why you didn't want me to take the blood for a locator spell?"

"Exactly! I won't reveal myself for a two-bit crime like this. Hopefully, we'll be out of town by tomorrow."

"I wish you hadn't said that." He grimaced. "It always feels like you jinx us when you say that."

They reached their building and she put her hand out to open the door when it was thrust open.

CHAPTER FIVE

Dick stared at the katana a fraction of an inch away from Betsy's face. "Lexi, you are not to kill Betsy. She's my dearest friend."

Lexi slid the blade into her pocket. "I was preparing to defend myself."

"Against me? The most dangerous thing I'll ever approach you with will be a cupcake." The woman laughed but it was a little strained.

Scott checked his watch. "Where are you two going? It's after two am."

The vampire extended his arm to his companion. "Betsy's never seen The French Quarter so I'm giving her a tour."

Betsy took his arm but before they walked away, she turned to Lexi. "What happened with the little girl?"

"It was a break-in at a creepy death museum. Someone stole…" She looked at Scott.

Scott rolled his eyes. "Marie Laveau."

"Marie Laveau's ring," she finished. "She was some kind of—"

Dick held a hand up. "I know who Marie Laveau was. Lexi, your education is somewhat lacking."

The older woman's eyes widened. "Did you catch the perp?"

Everyone looked at her.

"The perp?" Dick asked and fought to hide a smile.

"Yes, dear. The unsub." She seemed to be warming to her subject.

The vampire put his other hand over hers and addressed Lexi. "Marcel's snoring his little head off in the apartment. We collected our bags from the hotel and settled up. Come along, Nancy Drew."

"Have fun," Scott called from behind them as they headed up the street.

Betsy rested her head on Dick's arm for a few moments, then looked at him. "How long did you live here?"

"A few years. Not long. It's good to be back, though. New Orleans has a way of getting under your skin, even if the heat is somewhat uncomfortable for someone of my disposition."

They approached a street corner and he led them purposefully straight ahead. She glanced at him. "Where are we going?"

He patted her hand. "I think my oldest friend should meet some of my oldest silent friends."

They chatted as they walked through the streets while he pointed out hotels, stores, and bars he knew, although many had changed since he'd last been there. Finally, they reached a metal gate.

"A cemetery?" Betsy stopped abruptly.

"You're safe with me, dear. I like to check up on who's no longer with us since I was here last."

He guided her through the side gate and they walked along the narrow, tomb-lined paths.

The moon was almost full, which allowed her to read the tombstones as they passed. "Were the friends you're looking for all supernaturals?"

"Heavens, no. Some are, of course." He stopped facing a small family plot. "This is Marianne. I stayed with her while I waited for my house to be renovated. I see her son has joined her. He didn't like me very much—in fact, he assaulted me."

"He what? I hope you beat him senseless." Betsy shook her fist in the air.

"I couldn't catch him. He kicked me and ran away. He was quite fast for a five-year-old." Dick touched the stone plaque. "That was forty years ago. Forty-five is very young to die, isn't it?"

Betsy looked at the stone, then at him again. "You must have died around the same age."

Dick merely nodded.

Along the next aisle, they stopped before a large, ornate tomb. "This is Stephen and many of his ancestors. He was the alpha of a local shifter pack. I had tremendous respect for Stephen. Everyone did. He was fair and forward-thinking."

"He liked you too," a voice said behind them.

They turned toward it and he narrowed his eyes to stare at a woman with long hair he thought might be equal parts of gray and brown. She looked gaunt. "Geraldine? Why, you've barely changed."

"You're kind, but I think there have been one or two changes between twenty and sixty." She walked forward but stopped a little distance from them.

The vampire didn't move but he introduced the women. Betsy stepped up to the other woman and put her hand out. "It's lovely to meet a friend of William's."

Geraldine flicked her gaze briefly to him and they shared a look that said, "Humans, they haven't a clue," and she shook the proffered hand.

Dick looked around. "This is a strange place to find the living at such an hour."

The newcomer shrugged. "I'm contemplating my mortality and visiting old friends." She broke into a wracking cough and it took her a few seconds to regain her composure. "Are you here to choose a side?"

He smelled blood on her breath, took a handkerchief out, and stepped closer to her, holding it out like a white flag. "Good heavens, no. I'm trying to avoid whatever's going on and I certainly don't want to be here when this place finally erupts. I can't get out of here fast enough."

She took the handkerchief and wiped her mouth. "Did you know Kindred left?"

"I heard they're back already." He thought it might be prudent to bolster Lexi's fake Kindred identity.

Geraldine raised her eyebrows. "Really? I'm surprised. As I understand it, something has happened to draw them across the country, but it's not entirely an accident they left no one here."

Dick stepped to Betsy's side. "Do you think they're looking the other way? Leaving the city unprotected? But why?"

She held the handkerchief up but he gestured for her to keep it. She stuffed it into her pocket. "They aren't always as impartial as we'd like them to be."

"Well no, that's true, but who do you complain to —Congress?"

The woman barked a laugh and began to cough again. She yanked the handkerchief out.

"I think, in this instance, your concerns might be unfounded. I know what's been going on across the country and Kindred weren't even aware of it until it had mostly all blown over."

"Well, I've been wrong before. Time will tell." Geraldine walked forward and touched her family tomb. "So, do you plan to spend your final moments reminiscing in front of my father's tomb?"

"My final? Oh!" In his melancholy mood, he'd failed to consider the sun's imminent rise.

Her brow furrowed. "You don't have family here, do you?"

"No. No, I don't." He knew what she was asking—"Do you

have a family tomb to hop into?" Happily, the answer was no, but he didn't know what else to do. He didn't want anyone to know he could walk in the sun and hoped Betsy wouldn't say anything. A little disconcerted, he looked around. While he could reach cover at vamp speed, he wouldn't leave his friend there alone.

"I'm sure my father wouldn't forgive me if I allowed you to fry in front of him." Geraldine unscrewed a bolt and removed the front stone from her family tomb. It would have been heavy but even at sixty, her shifter strength made it appear as though it were no heavier than cardboard.

Dick looked inside the tomb with horror. His gaze darted about, looking for a reason to not have to climb in there wearing a designer suit.

"Come along dear, hop in. We can't have you flaming up, can we?" Betsy appeared to be enjoying it.

He glowered at her. "Yes, of course. Right." Reluctantly, he slid feet first onto the top shelf.

"There's a good man. I'll pop back for you at sunset, shall I?" His so-called friend could barely contain her glee.

Geraldine prepared to replace the stone. "You're lucky. They took the bricks from the front and pushed Dad down the back a few months ago when I got my diagnosis. I've had a reprieve of sorts so I won't be joining him quite yet, but it'll be soon enough."

"Geraldine, I'm sorry to hear that. Thank you so much for this. You're exactly like your father." He looked at Betsy, who still grinned unashamedly. "Betsy dear. Without the bricks on the face, the light will come in along the edges. I'll need you here to block the sun."

Her jaw dropped.

"In you hop." He patted the stone ledge.

With the shifter safely behind her, she gave him a withering look. She sighed and rolled her eyes to acknowledge that she knew she'd been caught by her smart mouth and climbed up.

Geraldine replaced the front stone. "Don't do anything in there to disgrace my father's memory."

"Geraldine!" Dick was horrified.

They listened to her laugh and cough as she walked away.

Betsy wriggled in an effort to get comfortable. Finally, she rested her head on his chest. "We won't be here until sunset, will we?"

"No. We'll give it half an hour or so, then make good our escape."

She stretched to touch the wall. "I think this would be the hardest part for me."

He looked down and spoke to the top of her head. "We don't usually sleep in tombs."

"Not that, silly." She slapped his shoulder, then sighed. "Everyone dying. Friends, family, loved ones. Making friends knowing you'll lose them. Falling in love, knowing—"

The vampire kissed the top of her head. "You've always had an incredible knack for getting to the heart of things."

She was silent for a moment before she asked, "What happened? In Europe."

"Oh, the usual story. Boy meets boy. Boy takes part in inadvisable practices and dies. Boy comes back."

"When you came back as your grandson, Harv and I used to talk about all the ways you were so similar to our William. But we'd talk about the differences too."

"I think people see what they want to see."

"No. I think in many ways, you are different. You were quite the hot-head, exuberant and excitable. When you returned as your grandson…" Betsy straightened suddenly and hit her head. "Ouch. What was that? Your heartbeat?"

Dick chuckled and rubbed her head. "It does now and then. I like to think that vampirism isn't a true death. It's merely…very close."

She settled again. "What will happen to you, when you die?"

"Do you mean heaven or hell?"

"No, you goose. I mean your body."

"Well, I recall you once told me you and Harv held a lovely memorial service for me. So that's already done. I suppose I'll simply blow away in the wind one day."

"I don't think so. I'll leave instructions with Lexi and Dolores that when you go, you're to be buried with us in the family plot. I think Harv would like that."

Dick was choked up. He knew, if Betsy could see in this dark place, she'd see tears welling in his eyes and cleared his throat. "Come on, she's gone. Let's get out of here. God knows what this has done to my suit."

"And my dress." Betsy shuffled out of the way to allow him access to the front.

"I suppose, but I care less about that." He unscrewed the bolt and peered through the brickwork at the top.

Satisfied that they were unobserved, he climbed out and lifted her to the ground.

She was laughing. "Dick, you really know how to show a girl a good time."

He smiled. "In my defense, showing girls a good time has never been my forté."

"Do you not mind being called Dick?"

"I'll tell you a secret but you must never tell Lexi." He paused until she nodded. "I rather like it. It's like being a secret agent with a new identity. Dolores will make me a new passport and driving license for my Dick identity when I've decided on a surname."

They dusted their clothes off as best they could and wandered toward the exit. Betsy read names out from the tombs as they went. "What about Trudeau. Dick Trudeau."

He tried it. "Dick Trudeau. No, too many hard consonants."

"Dick Nicholas?"

"Dick Nick?" He raised an eyebrow.

"Oh, good point. Ooh, here's a good one. Grayson. Dick Grayson. That sounds—"

"Familiar? Dick Grayson is the Boy Wonder. I am no one's Robin."

"You're kind of Lexi's Robin." She smiled.

"That's Scott. He is Lexi's Robin. I'm more like—"

"Batgirl?" Betsy laughed.

"Betsy!"

The vampire stopped at a tomb covered in writing with beads and other paraphernalia scattered at its base. "This is Marie Laveau's tomb."

She put a finger out and touched a marking of XXX. "Lipstick?" She frowned at her fingertip, which was now red.

"The three Xs are voodoo prayers to Marie. This is how people usually get her attention rather than stealing her jewelry. Do you have any requests while we're here?"

The woman patted the tomb. "I think I have everything I'll ever want and more than I could ask for." She turned to him. "Let's go to the apartment. It looks like we'll both sleep through the day."

As they walked through the Quarter, he mulled over Betsy's last response.

Women really are a mystery.

CHAPTER SIX

Three hours later, the morning was overcast and hot as the street cleaners made their way through the Quarter. They moved down sidewalks and swept disposable cocktail cups into the street to be gathered by street cleaning vehicles that moved slowly and loudly behind them.

Lexi and Scott entered Jackson Square.

"I heard it raining in the night. It belted down for all of ten minutes. Why is there no difference to the humidity? This can't be normal." She tried to adjust her leather vest as they walked.

A man in a business suit stared as he passed. She gave him her warning look and he averted his eyes.

They stopped roughly halfway across the width of the square and stood before the doors of the cathedral. She retrieved the photograph, looked from it to their current position, and estimated that they were roughly in the same place now as she had been all those years before.

In silence, she turned in a circle and scanned the area.

Scott looked from her to the cathedral doors and back again. "Anything?"

She turned the corners of her mouth down in an exaggerated

frown and shook her head. "Not a thing." Irritated, she shoved the picture into her pocket.

They continued to wander around the square. She turned to her companion and pretended not to notice the hostile looks she received from the fortune-tellers seated at tables, where they prepared their little street businesses for the day ahead. "Did Dolores get back to you about her contact here?"

"She's setting up a meeting and she'll call later this morning," he replied absently. He wasn't looking at faces and instead, stared at the tabletops as they passed.

"What are you looking at?" Lexi focused on the tables too.

"I'm curious to see which tarot decks and other forms of divination they use." He glanced at her before he returned to his curious study. "Professional curiosity."

Lexi pulled him out of the way of an oncoming bicycle. "Professional curiosity? Since when have you ever used props like cards or tea leaves? I didn't think that was the way of a mage and his sorcery."

"It's not really. They take magic from the earth and I take it from the air. We use it differently too, but it's essentially the same magic."

Scott turned away from the tables after receiving many suspicious looks. "I'll be happy to get out of here. God knows how the local Kindreds cope. These people are so hostile it makes me uncomfortable."

"Same here." Lexi adjusted her vest again. *In so many ways.* "Kindred are probably the ones to blame. I don't know how they run this town but I can guess."

As they turned onto Decatur, two men approached. The large one smiled at her to reveal a gold tooth and the other held a bottle and a rag. She glanced at the bottle and wondered if it was chloroform. The men moved directly toward them.

"Good morning, my friend." The large man addressed Scott. "I bet I can tell you where you got your shoes."

"I'm sorry?" He frowned in confusion.

"I can tell you the city, the state, and the exact name of the place." He smiled at the sorcerer in a friendly way that put Lexi's guard up.

He looked at his low-tops. They were regular Converse.

The man continued. "I can tell you where you got them. If I'm wrong, I'm gone."

She was about to tell the guy to take a hike when Scott grinned. "Okay."

"My name is Tyrone and this here is Julian. What's your name, my man?"

"Scott."

"Well, Scott. If I'm right, you'll tell me the truth, okay? Shake my hand." The man held his hand out and he shook it.

While they were shaking hands, the other man crouched and squibbed a creamy substance from the bottle onto the front of Scott's Converse.

"Hey!" The young man was surprised.

The man leaned toward Lexi's boots and she stepped back quickly. He glanced into her eyes and returned his attention to Scott's feet, took the rag, and polished his trainers.

Tyrone continued to talk. "I said I'd tell you where you got your shoes—the city, the state, and the exact place. Well, I can tell you, my friend, you got those shoes on your feet, in the city of New Orleans, in the state of Louisiana, and the exact place is right here on Decatur. That'll be forty dollars—twenty dollars each for the shoeshine." He flashed the gold tooth again.

"I didn't do the lady," Julian told his friend. The large man glanced at her and she simply inclined her head with her brow raised. He looked at Scott with a smile. "Twenty dollars."

The sorcerer's jaw dropped. He looked at Lexi and she smirked in response. As he focused on the man again, his cheeks colored. Then, to her surprise, he grinned. "You totally got me."

"Yes, sir, we did." Tyrone smiled.

Scott withdrew a twenty from his pocket and passed it to the guy. "I've paid more for a valuable lesson. Thank you, guys." He shook both their hands and they continued.

"Considering you basically got mugged, you look remarkably happy." Lexi's eyes narrowed.

He pointed across the street to the Café Du Mondé, "Beignets! I've been dying to try them."

As they crossed the street, a scream made her glance over her shoulder. Tyrone's pants were on fire. He yanked a pile of burning dollars from his pocket and dropped them wildly. While he patted the flames on his pants out, his friend stamped on the burning money, but the blaze didn't extinguish until all the money had turned to ash.

Scott skipped ahead of her and opened the café door. She raised an eyebrow at him as he smiled and looked at the overcast sky. "It looks like a beautiful day for learning, all round."

They ordered at the counter and waited until the coffee arrived alongside beignets, barely visible under a mountain of powdered sugar. Scott took one but made the rookie error of breathing in as he went to stuff it into his mouth. The result was the inhalation of a sizable portion of sugar and a coughing fit that drew the attention of everyone in the cafe.

"Good work, slugger." Lexi grinned.

He took a long sip of his coffee, then wiped his wet eyes.

She had been looking forward to trying the square sugar-laden donuts. While she'd seen them elsewhere, she'd always felt you had to try them for the first time in New Orleans. Now, she wondered if this *was* the first time. She could have been in this cafe, even in this seat, and still have no recollection of it.

It wasn't a pleasant thought and she took a breath—well out of range of the powdered sugar—and drew the tasty-looking morsel toward her mouth. She halted her hand a few inches away, suddenly aware of a small face very close to hers. Her gaze slid to the right. It was the young girl who'd found her the night before.

Lexi sighed and turned her face fully to the girl. "Is there some kind of tracking device on me that I have yet to find?"

The youngster put her hand on her jacket. "You have to come."

She looked at her beignet and then the girl. "I'm kind of having a moment here."

In response, she tugged at her sleeve. "They said you have to come."

"Listen." She replaced the beignet and turned in her seat. "We've looked at the crime scene. We're on the case, totally all over it—"

"It's not the museum." Scott stared intently at the youngster. "Someone's died, haven't they?"

The messenger nodded.

Shit!

"Can we get these to go, please?" Lexi asked the server. She grasped Scott's hand for a quick boost of magical energy.

The two friends left the café and followed their young guide. They neared the crime scene and she was aware of Scott staring as she slid a finger down the front of her vest, then sucked powdered sugar from it. "What? I missed it."

He raised an eyebrow and shook his head. "Nothing. Are we going up?"

"I'll go first. You check the gawkers." She looked at the crowd of locals who had gathered. Once again, she met the gaze of the man in the cowl and turned to her friend. "Make sure you speak to Dreadlock Gandalf over there."

Scott looked up. "Who?"

When she turned to point at the man, there was no sign of him. "This town is so creepy." She shook her head, dusted sugar from her vest, and passed the beignet bag to him. "They were so good. I left you one." With one last swipe of her mouth, Lexi headed into the building and up to the second-floor apartment. She stared at the corpse and examined it from every angle as she tried to work out what was supposed to go where. Hands down, she would swear she'd never seen a corpse as fucked up as this one, and given the condition she'd left some creatures in, that was saying something. When someone entered the room, she ignored them.

A man spoke from behind her. "It amazes me how you people always get here before—whoa!"

She glanced at the newcomer. The tall, handsome, African American man gazed slack-jawed at the body. He pulled a Dictaphone from an inside pocket, which revealed a glimpse of his police badge. She kicked herself mentally for not preparing for this. He would ask for her name and ID. Things were about to get awkward. She allowed her thumb to stray to the scar in case she needed to send him to sleep.

He stepped beside her. In her peripheral vision, she could see him tilt his head in the same way she'd done. When he lifted the Dictaphone, he merely opened and closed his mouth as though unsure where to start. Finally, he began to speak into the device. "Male victim, late teens or early twenties, African American—"

Lexi passed him two wallets hanging side by side from the blade of her stiletto knife and he stopped speaking. He took them in a gloved hand, flipped one open, then the other.

Clicking the recorder back on, he continued "Jamal Simpson, nineteen. Torso has been completely splayed. Front and back of the body are both visible. We might be looking for a butcher."

She turned to face him. "A butcher?"

The cop nodded as he switched his recorder off. "You can't tell from this angle, but I'm willing to bet his spine's missing."

"It's not missing," she protested.

He rolled his eyes. "You know you're not supposed to disturb the scene."

"I haven't touched him. It's over there." She pointed a thumb behind her.

The man turned and grimaced at the gory display of a spine hung from a floor lamp.

"Well, I assume it's his." Lexi shrugged. "You said a butcher."

The cop turned to the body again. "Someone big and very strong, given the strength required to rip out a human spine. He's been spatchcocked, also known as butterflying. It's usually done to chickens. In fact, I do it to chickens when I'm barbecuing, but I don't think I'll do that for a while. The backbone is removed, the back ribs pulled apart, and the breastplate flattened."

"Oh yes, I see the bloody footprints." She nodded and he continued. "Then the legs and wings—or in this case, arms—are spread to allow fast, even cooking."

Lexi frowned. "How big is the oven here? And what do you think the white stuff is?" She inspected the smears of white over the boy's skin.

"It's not mixed with the blood, so I'd say that's an oil-based theatrical paint. He's clearly an amateur or he'd use flour if he was going to use anything." He looked at the floor and poked at a pair of short shorts and a spaghetti string top with the toe of his shoe. "Is there any sign of the girl?"

She shook her head. "Amy? No, but I only just got here."

He looked at the ID and confirmed the girl's name with a nod.

A cop called from outside the room. "Detective Broullard, one coming in."

Lexi felt Scott's presence. The cop turned to him. "Who are you?"

"Scott. I'm—"

"He's with me," she explained, then diverted his attention before he asked exactly who she was. "There seem to be a few ritual pieces here."

"I'm happy to leave that to you if I can. Of course, it'll have to be bagged and tagged but I'll leave it for you to work your mojo."

Broullard moved across the room to get a closer look at the spine, which gave Scott a full view of the corpse.

"Oh! Oh!" He lurched out the door.

The man's gaze followed his rapid retreat. "What's with him?"

"I'm training him." Lexi studied the grisly scene, taking in the bowls, cups, beads, and bones scattered about the floor.

Broullard gestured toward the corpse. "So, is this one of yours or one of ours?"

Yours or ours. She had assumed, by this point, that he was directly connected to Kindred in some way. It seemed the police there had a working relationship with Kindred she'd not experienced elsewhere. Many of her ex-employer's organization were police officers but their Kindred affiliation was certainly not in the open and they never trusted non-Kindred officers.

"Well?" She glanced toward the door.

"Ours," Scott's muffled voice said from the hallway.

"Okay, I'll wait outside. You have about a half-hour until the uniforms get here. I'll let you do your thing." Broullard headed to the door.

"Be careful you don't step in the vomit," she called,

The cop looked around the floor. "What vomit?"

A moment later, they heard the sound of Scott throwing up in the hallway.

He tilted his head toward the door. "First day on the job?"

"Something like that." Lexi rolled her eyes and refocused on the corpse.

She waited for the cops to retreat, then stuck her head out the door. "Are you ready?"

Scott nodded. He still looked miserably green but followed her into the apartment.

The sorcerer looked around the room and his gaze traced the blood spatter trails up the walls and drapes, clearly trying to avoid the body. "Strange, there are no mirrors in this room. I don't see anything shiny enough to get a playback." He waved his hands experimentally. "And not much dust." He lowered his hands and sighed. "They don't make this easy. All right, then."

He held his arm out with his palm up and muttered a few words, and a ball of light grew in his hand. It elevated and spun above the body.

"What's it doing?" The light moved so fast, Lexi couldn't maintain her focus on it.

"It's following the path of anything magical in the room."

They watched as it bounced across the room from Jamal, over to the spine, back to the victim, through the couch and finally, it rocketed out the side of the couch, significantly smaller, and into a large cupboard at the bottom of a wooden shelving unit. It didn't come out.

She turned to her friend. "What does that mean?"

Scott put his finger to his lips and pointed at the cupboard.

Her eyes widened and she hurried to the apartment door. "Broullard?" She dug her hand into her dimensional pocket and drew the katana.

The cop entered and raised his eyebrows at the blade. He opened his mouth to speak but when she signaled silently to the cupboard, he nodded and drew his gun.

She motioned for Scott to stay back and she and the officer crept forward.

Broullard yanked the door open and she brought the katana to within an inch of the girl's face. Her eyes were wide but there was no reaction.

"Amy, I presume." She withdrew the sword.

"Is she dead?" Scott leaned around her.

"No, catatonic." She felt the girl's neck and found a pulse but couldn't see any injuries. Amy was curled in her underwear and covered in blood, but none of it seemed to be hers. Lexi looked at Scott. "Can you bring her out of it?"

"I'm not sure this is the best place for that." He indicated the mangled corpse without looking at it. "If she sees that, her mind will probably close up again."

"Okay, let's see if we can get her out of this cupboard first." She took the girl's right arm and Broullard leaned forward to take her left one but jumped back and struck his head on the top of the cupboard.

"Shit!" He gestured to Amy's other side as he rubbed his head.

When she leaned into the cupboard, she saw why he had jumped. The young woman's hand was clenched tightly around a gore-covered machete.

CHAPTER SEVEN

Lexi finished describing the scene. She'd left many of the details out in front of Betsy, who was still clearly horrified.

"That's simply awful. What happens to her now?" The older woman shuddered. She stood from her seat at the table on the balcony overlooking the street and took her coffee cup inside.

Scott put his feet onto the chair she had vacated. "They were able to walk her out of the apartment but she wasn't there mentally. She's in the hospital now, cuffed to the bed until the scene gets processed."

Betsy turned. "But I thought the detective said she wouldn't have been strong enough to do that."

He nodded. "He thinks she's a victim but with no other suspects, they have to be careful. Personally, I think it was her. There was magic all over the scene but no indication of it entering or leaving the room. The trail faded and stopped around Amy."

Dick was seated against the wall in the room and remained out of sight until the sun went down. "What will you do? I'm sure Kindred won't be gone for much longer."

Lexi slapped her friend's arm. "Feet!" He put them down

hastily. "It's a murder so I can't not investigate it. If it wasn't Amy who did it, there's a psycho on the loose."

Betsy washed her cup and put it on the sink. "But isn't that the job for the police? If they have the girl and the body, surely they'll investigate it."

Scott turned in his chair to look at her. "Incredibly strong magic was present in that room. It's not a job for the regular police to investigate alone. I guess that's why this Broullard guy is on it."

The vampire spoke from behind the wall. "So, what's next?"

"I came here for a reason. Dolores has sent us the name of her contact, so I'll see her before I do anything else."

At an unexpected knock, they all looked toward the door.

"That was my door." Dick stood and moved to the peephole.

Lexi walked across to join him. She mouthed, "Who is it?"

He looked at her, shrugged, and moved aside to allow her to look. All she could see was the back of the man's head and a key in his hand. She waited until he had it in the lock before she opened her door quickly.

"Can I help you?" she snapped.

The man jumped and turned with shock on his face. "I'm... I clean these apartments."

She studied him suspiciously. "What's your name?"

The guy looked into the corner and said "Erm...Mike."

It was clear he was lying, and not very well. She looked into the hallway to check for anyone else, then stepped out. "Well, Erm-Mike, that apartment is occupied by someone who likes to sleep late."

"Oh, I see. Well, I'll come back later." He turned to walk away.

"Erm-Mike?" Lexi leaned against the wall with her arms folded.

He paused and looked over his shoulder.

She smiled sweetly. "Don't you want to clean this apartment?"

"Oh, well..."

"And where's your mop and bucket?"

The guy ran.

Lexi touched the scar briefly and a second later, Erm-Mike sprawled on his face. As she stepped toward him, she felt a breeze when Dick moved rapidly behind her before his apartment door clicked shut. *Damn, that vamp's fast.*

She held the guy by his shirt collar and sat him against the wall. Her grin widened as she glanced at his feet.

The old shoelace trick.

The handsome young man was clearly petrified and looked down, baffled by the fact that his laces were inexplicably tied together.

Scott stepped into the hallway. "He doesn't seem to have the disposition of a cat burglar, does he?"

"I'm not a thief." He blushed. "I'm a fan."

Lexi's eyebrows raised.

"I was in the bar when he arrived last night. I'm a donor there. I've heard of Mr. Levine and came to offer my services."

Dick shouted through his apartment door. "Who's out there at what-the-fuck-o'clock?"

"See, you woke him." She shook her head. "Come back at a decent time."

"Midnight," the vampire shouted quickly.

She released the man's shirt, returned her apartment, and closed the door.

Dick returned after his visitor had left. "What will you do next about the case?"

Lexi shrugged. "Broullard seemed to think we would know what the voodoo paraphernalia was for. I suppose it's the kind of thing the local Kindred see all the time, but I couldn't tell you what they were trying to do."

He frowned as he poured himself a drink. "Do you know what ingredients they used?"

When she shook her head, he added. "I'll come and take a look. I might see something helpful. If I can't help, I know a guy."

Deep in thought, he held the glass against his bottom lip before he finally took a sip.

She shook her head. "If my legacy senses were better, I could have given you ingredients and quantities."

Betsy glanced at her watch. "I must get ready. I'm going for a walk to soak up the atmosphere." The woman stepped to the mirror on the wall and began to brush her dark, shiny hair. She glanced at Lexi through the reflection a few times before she finally asked, "What exactly is a legacy?"

Her gaze darted around to avoid direct contact. "It's kind of a diplomat."

Dick spat his bourbon across the room and made choking sounds.

The older woman patted his back and turned to her. "I'm not naïve, dear. I know you killed people for Kindred. What I'm asking is how you become legacies and mages."

Lexi smiled. "For the record, I also once rescued a kitten. The job involved more than running around poking people with pointy things."

"Not much more," the vampire muttered.

She gave him a hard stare, then turned to Betsy.

"Kindred also has the ability to send people to The Hollows. It's a prison in its own dimension so they don't always kill transgressors. To answer your question, sorcerers are born. You can't acquire the ability to be one like you can with other magic. Once a sorcerer has been trained to a certain level within Kindred, they are given the title of mage. There are a couple of ways to make a legacy. We can be born directly of the bloodline from a legacy parent, or the legacy blood is introduced to our DNA in a ritual and gives us... Well, it's *supposed* to give us properties of the supernatural creatures who offered their blood for use in the ritual."

"So that's vampires and shifters and fae?" Betsy put the hair-brush down and picked up a pair of earrings.

Lexi smiled. "Yes, and dozens more that you've probably never heard of."

Scott held a finger up. "And one drop of blood from a sorcerer who disguised himself as a witch after being told sorcerers couldn't participate in the ritual because we're too awesome."

She rolled her eyes. "*Not* a single drop of sorcerer blood because legacies are already blood-bound to sorcerers. It was decided that would upset the balance."

"Okay, yes," he conceded, "that part might be a myth—"

"That sorcerers tell other sorcerers. Not one legacy has ever shown sorcerer tendencies." She shook her head at him.

"But if a legacy and a mage have a child, won't the child have sorcerer blood?" the woman asked.

"The offspring of a blood-bonded couple will either be a sorcerer or a legacy or possibly merely a regular human child—" She stopped speaking when she realized Betsy's expression had changed to one of sadness. "What?"

The woman turned to the mirror and once again looked at Lexi's reflection as she put the earrings in. "Maybe that's what happened to you. You could be the child of a mage and a legacy who was born human."

"If that were true, where are my real parents?" She sighed. "But it's not true, the part about being born fully human. I do have slightly enhanced abilities."

Betsy nodded. "So, the alternative is that the ritual didn't work as well with you. Do you know why that could have been?"

"I've never heard of it ever going wrong with anyone else. They told me I was a runaway who elected to go through the legacy ritual, but they lie so I don't know if that's even true. I've met a few other legacies. Some are so connected to the legacy blood in their veins that they can almost shift or move like vamps or sing like sirens."

The older woman turned away from the mirror and faced her, tilting her head. "Do you think the man in the photograph might be your father?"

She shrugged and turned away. Betsy was too perceptive.

The sun had finally made an appearance later in the afternoon, and Lexi fidgeted with her leather vest again as she strode along the sidewalk with Scott. "How far to this place?"

"It's on the next street, I think." Scott took his cell out, opened the maps app, and flicked the little blue cursor. It careened off the screen and hovered ahead of them with its little arrow pointing right.

"Nifty trick." She smiled. He hated it when she used the word "trick" to describe his magic.

He rolled his eyes.

They entered Thought and Memory, a dark little magic and witchcraft store. He immediately began to poke around in baskets and on shelves. A young man with a long, bushy beard shoved a box of sage sticks onto a shelf and approached them. "Can I help you?"

"Could I speak to Anne Bird, please? Tell her it's—"

"I know who she is. Back to work, James." The woman entered from the back of the store. She had long blonde hair and moved confidently toward them. James continued to stack the shelves, while Anne turned to the door she'd walked through. "Sam?"

A voice responded from the room beyond. "Yes, Mom?"

"Where's that box?"

"What bo—" A young woman stuck her head out and took one look at Lexi. Her face darkened. "Oh, *that* box. It's on the shelf behind you under the divining rods." She disappeared into the room again.

Anne went to a shelf behind the checkout and picked up a box about the size of a ream of paper. "Here it is. If you don't mind leaving, I don't want people to see you in here. You're bad for business." She glanced at Scott, her eyes narrowed. He replaced the crystals he'd intended to buy and stepped out of the store.

"Well, thanks." Lexi shrugged, turned away, and followed him.

"Honestly, I feel like I have a big sign on my back saying *Kindred scum*." Lexi glanced over her shoulder to where the proprietor stared at her through the window. "Let's get back to the others."

When they reached the third floor, Lexi darted back onto the staircase, pulling Scott with her, and mouthed, "The apartment door's open."

He whispered a reply. "I gave Betsy a key."

"Why?"

"I don't need it and she likes the balcony." He shrugged.

She rolled her eyes and continued carefully. Sure enough, the woman was on the balcony with a glass of lemonade. She'd removed the enchanted necklace and was an eighty-year-old again who gazed onto the street.

Scott stepped outside. "Hi, Betsy. How are you?"

"I'm very well. It's a little hot out here but the flowers are lovely." She touched a tendril of blooms that trailed from the basket above. "Help me in, dear."

He offered her his arm and she rose slowly, making pained noises.

She sat on a dining chair indoors and fanned herself. "I expect you're wondering why I'm fifty years older again."

As he replied, he closed the balcony door so the air-con could regulate. "I assumed you didn't want to let yourself get lost in the magic and forget who you are."

"Clever boy." Betsy smiled.

"Clever girl," he countered. "I gave it to you because I believe you are wise enough not to be taken over by the magic. The enchantment is for others, not yourself. Of course, there's the benefit of losing the aches and pains but don't overdo it."

Lexi smiled at the two of them. She plucked the shuriken from her vest and sliced through the tape on the box.

The older woman looked at the sharp, intricately designed object. "I do like your little murder brooch. It's very pretty."

She raised an eyebrow. "I think we'll have to watch you."

With a grin, she put the shuriken onto the counter and flipped the box lid open.

"I don't understand." Utterly baffled, she lifted a dark-red fabric vest out and held it up.

"That's pretty, dear." Betsy stretched to feel the fabric. "Linen, I think. It looks more comfortable than the leather one."

Lexi frowned. "I expected documents."

The other woman leaned over the box. "Is there anything else in there? Maybe the documents are hidden to mislead prying eyes."

"No." She lifted the tissue paper to make sure before she looked at Scott. "Is there an enchantment on it?"

He put a hand over the box. "Nope." He took the vest and held it up. "It seems a little heavy for linen." With a small frown, he slid two fingers into a little pocket in the front, pulled a key out, and passed it to her.

She turned it in her hand but saw no distinguishing markings on it. "I'll have to take it back. She's mixed me up with a customer. Maybe she does alterations on the side."

The sorcerer looked more closely at the fabric. "Can I see your shuriken?"

Lexi passed it to him. "Be careful. I don't want to have to pay for this."

He held it next to the vest and let go. It snapped to a hidden magnet in the garment. "There are a few magnets along the front and magnetized pockets for blades, which explains why it's heavy. I think this was definitely meant for you."

She held the key up. "But why hide the key in a vest? And how is a key without a lock supposed to help?"

Scott rolled his eyes and tutted. "I think we're being dense."

"Speak for yourself." Dick walked through the door.

Lexi held her palms up. "Does everyone have a key to this place?"

The vampire waved the key in his hand. "The young man who tried to enter my apartment had a master key. It fits both locks. So, why is everyone but me dense?"

"Dolores must have sent the vest," Scott explained. "Mrs. Bird put the key in it. Try it on. I bet it fits."

She removed six little knives and a length of garrote wire from the lining of the leather vest and tugged at the hem in preparation to lift it off.

The sorcerer spun away, and Dick rolled his eyes and turned.

"Okay, you can look. This is fantastic." Lexi turned in the linen vest.

"It's lined and feels so cool. What a revelation." She clicked the ornate shuriken into place on the front. "This material's amazing. I need to find out if they do pants in this."

"Yes, I *think* they do pants in linen." Dick drawled with sarcasm. He shook his head. "I need to dress for dinner. Then we can head to your crime scene and I can be back in time for my new little friend."

Her brow creased. "I thought you were on the blood bags."

"There's no sense in looking a gift horse in the mouth." He grinned. "He smelled very healthy."

"I'll get ready too." Betsy walked slowly to the other apartment.

Dick watched her go. "That woman is remarkable. If she were a man, I'd marry her."

Scott laughed. "Don't tell her that or she'll ask for a new necklace to help her grow things she ought not to grow."

The vampire's eyes widened. "Scott! She was married to my best friend."

"It never ceases to amaze me how the object of someone's affections can remain so oblivious." The young man shook his head. "If I were to guess, I'd say she was in love with you long before your friend."

The other man shook his head firmly. "That's positively ridiculous. Betsy and Harv are one of the greatest love stories of a generation. All the girls wanted Harv and all the boys wanted Betsy. She had the looks of Lauren Bacall, the grace of Audrey Hepburn, and the humor of Doris Day." He turned to face Scott. "And if you say, "who?" so help me I'll—"

"Calm down. I've heard of the middle one," the sorcerer assured him.

"But you always looked like you," Betsy said as she entered as a woman in her thirties in a silk dressing gown. She went to the table at the mirror and retrieved her hairbrush. "Better looking than Clark, classier than Cary, and probably more gay than Rock." She patted Dick's face before she retreated to the other apartment again.

Five minutes later, she was back. "The bathroom's all yours."

They sat at a table in the Napoleon House restaurant and looked at the menu.

"Have I turned into an eighty-year-old again?" Betsy asked.

Scott looked up. "No. Why?"

She pinched the bridge of her nose. "I can't see a word on this menu."

"It is a little dim in here." Lexi agreed and glanced at the ceiling.

"The lighting in here is more a hint of light—a suggestion for atmospheric purposes." Dick took the menu and read it to the older woman.

When he reached Jambalaya, she called a halt. "That's the one for me!"

Lexi and Scott ordered po' boys, and the vampire asked for a double Jack Daniels and "keep them coming."

Betsy put her hand on Dick's arm. "You won't be drunk at a crime scene, will you? I'm sure that's terribly bad form."

"Darling, I'm undead. It's impossible to incapacitate me."

Scott grinned. "Except that time—you know, when Caleb's vampire pal almost cubed you."

She scowled. "That monster."

"Sorry, Betsy." The young man's brow drew down in a guilty expression.

"It's all right dear." She smiled at him and turned to Dick. "Do you miss food?"

"Not really. I did for the first ten or twenty years, though."

The meal arrived and Scott picked up his po' boy. "I think I'd miss it forever." He tucked in but dropped half the contents of the sandwich down his front.

Lexi stared at him. "At least as much as you miss your mouth."

Scott flicked a finger at the crime scene tape across the door. A further whisper opened the lock and the door swung open.

Betsy's eyes widened. "That's awfully clever and so useful."

Lexi turned to glance at her, then at Scott.

He received the unspoken message. "You two go up. Betsy and I will keep a lookout."

The woman darted him a withering look. "I have a strong stomach."

He frowned. "I haven't. I threw up the last time I was in there. You're staying to look after me."

"Oh, you dear boy." Betsy took his arm and patted his shoulder.

Scott leaned through the door behind Lexi as she entered the building. "Take a look down the couch. The light went wherever the magic was, and it went through that couch. Something might be stashed there." She nodded and headed up the stairway with Dick.

She touched her scar. "Open." The door to the apartment flew open and banged against the wall.

"Jesus! Isn't there a dial on that thing?" The vampire put his hand over his chest. "My heart."

"Which doesn't beat." She smirked. "Drama queen!"

He turned to her. "I resent that remark."

"What would you prefer?"

"Sensitive queen."

She rolled her eyes. "Get in."

They entered the apartment and wandered through to the living room. The body was gone, thank goodness. She glanced at the lamp in the corner, relieved that the spine had also been removed.

Dick walked to the center of the room. "That's an enormous quantity of blood."

"No snacking," Lexi warned.

He screwed his face up. "Seriously, would you eat food off the floor?"

"Five-second rule." She shrugged.

"Animal." He shuddered and sniffed the air several times.

Lexi opened drawers and poked around on shelves. "What can you smell?"

"Well, I can detect at least three hallucinogens."

She held a black satin bag up and shook it next to her ear. "Anything else?"

"Blood, star anise, blood, mandrake, blood, and mugwort."

"Very good." The unexpected voice spoke from the door.

It was the disappearing Gandalf from the crime scenes. Lexi's katana was in her hand in an instant.

Dick stepped between them in a fraction of a second. "Please don't decapitate Joseph. Marcel's taken quite a shine to him."

With a dramatic sigh, she put the sword away. "This voodoo stuff makes me antsy."

The vampire smiled at her with no sincerity whatsoever. "What a charming thing to say to a voodoo priest."

She studied the new arrival suspiciously. "Joseph and I keep almost bumping into each other."

"Yes, I am quite eager to make your acquaintance." The man's voice was deep, rich, and southern. Lexi couldn't shake the feeling that something about her amused him.

Dick stepped aside. "Joseph, Lexi. Lexi, Joseph." To his friend, he said. "Lexi used to be with our Kindred friends but recently had a change of heart and decided to spread her wings."

Joseph nodded. "Ah! I'm sure that went down well. Are you planning to stay in New Orleans, Lexi?"

She answered honestly. "No, I'm planning to get the hell out of here before the local Kindred return."

He grinned. "That's a shame. It's a family get-together I'd pay money to see."

"So, what were they up to in here?" She indicated the ritual area in the room.

"Young Jamal has only been in town for a couple of weeks. He and his pretty young friend have done the rounds and tried to ingratiate themselves with the local priests and priestesses. They were tourists. I didn't detect the capacity for anything like this in either of them."

"You mean murder?" Lexi went to the couch, intending to ease her hand down the back of it, but paused and stared at it.

I've battled demons but I still don't want to stick my hand down the back of this couch in case it's icky.

Joseph shook his head. "I mean power. Something powerful and quite evil has been in this room."

"Did you hear how Jamal died?" Dick asked.

The other man nodded. "I've spoken to the detective. It seems quite…exotic."

Lexi opened a cupboard, glanced in, and closed it again. "And where might this evil something be now?"

He spread his arms. "It could be anywhere. I'm sure your mage friend could locate it."

She returned to the satin bag and upended it onto a side table. It was a pile of bones. When she moved to swipe them into the bag, a strong hand caught her wrist. Joseph studied the bones. He glanced at her, raised his eyebrows, and laughed a deep, loud belly laugh, then walked out the door.

A little startled, she narrowed her eyes. The guy was annoying. She followed him through the door to ask what was so funny, but when she turned into the hallway, he was nowhere to be seen.

"Seriously," she snapped as she entered the room again. "That is one creepy fucking dude."

Dick smiled. "He's very nice when you get used to him."

Lexi returned to the couch and lifted the cushions. "We'll have to speak to Amy, won't we?"

"It looks that way." He looked at the couch. "Is there nothing in the couch?"

"Not even a quarter." She pushed the cushion into place again.

He raised an eyebrow. "I've never heard of a couch without a quarter hiding in there somewhere."

They headed out and down the stairs.

Betsy greeted them. "Interesting. Two went in and three came out."

Their two friends stood beside Joseph.

"I was introducing myself," the man said jovially. He turned to the older woman and bowed. "Good evening, little mother, you look extraordinarily well."

Her hand went involuntarily to her necklace.

"Ah, the necklace." He turned to Scott and nodded appreciatively. "Nicely done."

Lexi felt a tug at her side. She turned to see the young girl had found her again. "You have to be kidding me. Don't you have a curfew?"

Joseph held a hand out. "Hello, Agatha."

"Hi, Joseph." The kid held his hand without hesitation.

"Suffer the little children to come unto me, and forbid them not; for theirs is the kingdom of Heaven." He patted her cheek. "You need her, don't you?"

She nodded her head and they both looked at Lexi.

"Another one." Scott's shoulders slumped. It wasn't a question.

"Do you need me?" Dick asked.

Lexi shook her head. "No, it's late and, as I recall, you have an arrangement."

Betsy touched her arm. "May I wait in your apartment, dear? I'd like to enjoy the balcony for a while."

She smiled. "Of course. And if you prefer not to room with a sleazy vampire, you could stay with us."

Her gaze drifted to Joseph and she regarded him with a questioning eyebrow.

He sniffed the air. "I'll be around."

"We'll see you later," she assured Betsy and turned to Joseph. He was gone. "How does he do that?"

Scott shrugged. "Probably the same way I do."

"Yes, but it's not creepy when you do it."

Once again, they followed the girl through the dark streets.

CHAPTER EIGHT

Dick opened the door of the apartment, well aware that Betsy was across the hall and peered through the peephole to get a glimpse of the young man. He stood with his fingers twisting nervously and wore a Saints hoodie and jeans. The vampire studied him for a moment. "You must be Mike."

"Actually, it's Peter. Sorry. I panicked when I saw her earlier. I've seen her around but not up close and personal like that. I thought I would mess myself." He gave an apologetic shrug.

"Don't worry, Peter, she affects us all that way. Well, come on in." He stepped aside to allow him in, then winked at the spy hole before he closed the door.

He headed straight to the kitchen, opened a cupboard, and pulled out a bottle of Jack. "Would you like a drink?" he called. "I have bourbon or tea."

"No thank you," Peter responded. "I just had a couple with friends."

He's not exactly the life and soul of the party, is he?

Dick poured himself a large drink and walked in to find his visitor in exactly the same position he'd left him in. "Well, it seems I have catching up to do, chin-chin."

Peter smiled. "Penis."

He choked on his drink. "Pardon?"

"Chin-chin is Japanese for penis."

The vampire struggled to lower his eyebrows. "Well. I did not know that. In fact, it's remarkable that in all my years, that hasn't come up before. Have you eaten? I don't want you fainting on me."

"Yes, I'm fine. Thank you."

Dick led Peter through to the living room and gestured to the couch. "Great! I'm ravenous, Take a seat."

His visitor complied but he noticed the man's heart lurch when he said the word "ravenous." He decided he should probably slow things somewhat.

As non-threateningly as he could, he sat on the other side of the couch. "So, Peter. You said you were a fan. Of vampires in general?"

Suddenly, the young man perked up. "No, your movies. I think they're great."

What an astute young man. I was completely wrong about him.

"Peter, we will get on like a house on fire. Tell me, what's your favorite?"

"*A Long Dark Night in Hollywood.*"

He frowned. "But I die at the end of that one."

"I know. It always makes me cry when she holds your hand to her cheek and says, "Don't go, Johnny, don't go," and as you slip away, she doesn't see your other hand open and the diamond ring falls through the gap in the floorboards."

"I had to drop that goddam ring about a hundred times before it finally slipped through the—"

The vampire straightened quickly and Peter looked like he might have a heart attack. "Stay right where you are. I'll be back in a jiffy."

Humming "Tonight" from *West Side Story*, he hurried into the bedroom, opened a drawer in the big trunk, and flicked through a pile of DVDs before he drew one out and closed the drawer. He walked through the room and dropped a copy of *A Long Dark Night in Hollywood* onto the couch. "Be a dear and put that on. We can watch it for old times' sake." He moved to the kitchen, took a pack of Betsy's popcorn out, and threw it into the microwave. While it popped, he texted Lexi.

I have a theory.

Five minutes later, he was back on the sofa. Peter shoveled handfuls of popcorn into his mouth with one hand while he held his wrist out. Both had their gazes fixed on the movie in companionable silence.

Dick was unaware that anything was wrong until the bowl slid from the man's lap and scattered popcorn across the floor as he slumped.

"Peter?" The vampire checked his watch. They'd only been going seven minutes but he could hear the man's heart slowing.

Alarmed, he jumped to his feet to help him, but the moment he stood, he felt light-headed. He swayed and fell heavily. While not quite unconscious, he couldn't move when the door opened.

"Get Peter out. He'll be dead in an hour if he's not already. Drop him in a dumpster somewhere."

"What about the vamp?"

"I put enough roofies in Peter's drinks to fell an ox. Lorenzo wants us to take him to the roof and tie him up. He'll meet the sun in a few hours."

Dick began to lose consciousness.

"Why not chop his head off now and get it over and done with?"

Lexi stared at the body. "So where's his head?"

Broullard exhaled sharply and shrugged.

She looked around. "This is the smallest bathroom I've ever

seen. How do you behead someone in such a tiny space? The logistics are a nightmare." She noticed that he stared at her from her peripheral vision. "Like you didn't think it too. So, out with it. Why am I here?"

The cop pointed at the body. "This gentleman was Ambrose Jackson. His wife, Cora, does housekeeping for an agency that services several vacation apartments in the city."

The penny dropped and she nodded. "Let me guess—Jamal's place?"

"Correct."

He handed her a framed photograph of the couple on a vacation—a happy, smiling African American man with his loving white wife. "Could it be racially motivated?"

"They've been married for thirty years. The neighbors say they haven't had that kind of trouble for at least ten."

Lexi handed him the picture. "And the wife?"

Broullard shook his head. "She hasn't been seen but she had a key to Jamal's apartment."

She immediately followed what she suspected was the detective's train of thought. "You think this housekeeper could have let herself in when the two of them baked and butchered Jamal. Then Amy woke from a drug-addled stupor and found her boyfriend scrambled?"

"Spatchcocked. It looks like the most likely scenario. Simply because they were practicing voodoo at the time doesn't mean that caused his death."

"Okay…so you think she then came home and decapitated her husband." She peered into the little vanity sink at a blood-covered steak knife. "With a steak knife? This can't possibly be the murder weapon." She glanced at the body. "I'll admit it's not the cleanest cut but I'm sure you'd have to be built like Arnie to take someone's head off with an old steak knife."

They walked down the hall past piles upon piles of boxes that lined the wall. "What's all this?" Lexi asked and gestured at them.

"Stolen goods. It appears Mr. and Mrs. Jackson had a little side business—actually, I think they had a few side businesses. This stuff is everywhere. Games consoles, iPhones, there's a foot-high pile of counterfeit currency in the bedroom, a stash of narcotics in the kitchen, and we found an undocumented illegal in the back bedroom who says she hasn't left the building for over a year. They didn't treat her very well."

Her brows drew together in puzzlement. "Why did the wife work as a cleaner? No, let me guess, it was part of their victim selection process."

"Again, correct."

"Is there any indication they practiced voodoo?" She poked around the shelves and looked at him when he didn't respond. He looked from her to the wall, his expression a little sarcastic.

She turned and noticed the large painting of Marie Laveau on the wall.

"Oh, right. Duh." She stepped to the window and looked out, then turned to the door. "Where the hell is Scott?"

"I told them not to let him in. I don't want him puking all over the crime scene again."

"Fair enough." She nodded. "Listen, we'll have to speak to Amy. We'll go in the morning if that's okay with you."

Broullard stared at her for a few seconds. "I must say I like this whole new Kindred approach. It's much easier to work with."

Don't get used to it.

He took a notepad out, scribbled a few lines, and ripped the page out to hand it to her. "That's the hospital room."

"Great, thanks. I'll head off now. I'd like to get a couple of hours of sleep." She headed down the staircase to where Scott waited for her.

He shrugged dramatically. "They wouldn't let me in."

Lexi squeezed past the cop on the door. "You don't look disappointed about that."

"I'm not. I don't like to see the evil things people do to each other."

"You and me both." She took her cell out and read the screen. "Dick has a theory."

"About what?"

She shrugged. "Who knows. I won't ask."

"Why not?"

"Because he's being intentionally vague," she snipped as she put the cellphone in her pocket again.

***

Betsy was asleep on the couch when they returned. Her eyes opened sleepily as Scott closed the door.

He winced. "Sorry. I tried not to disturb you."

She sat quickly. "It's all right. What time is it?"

Lexi consulted the clock. "A little after three. Don't tell me Dick's dinner is still in there."

"I have no idea. I decided to rest my eyes and dropped off immediately."

Marcel jumped off a chair, ran to the door, and sat beside it as he yipped sharply.

"I'll take him." Lexi took the lead from the table.

"I'll accept your offer of the other bed." Betsy headed to the second bedroom and the younger woman opened the front door.

When she and Marcel entered the hallway, she considered knocking on Dick's door. She was less than impressed that he'd left Betsy feeling like she couldn't go back to the apartment.

When they reached the stairway, the puppy darted up the first two steps leading to the roof access and ate something from the floor. She tried to wrestle it from his mouth and realized it was popcorn. "You don't mind floor food, do you, boy?" She turned to walk down but he whined and stared upward. "There's no more, come on." She pulled him away and he followed reluctantly.

Lexi woke to a welcome smell. She crept over Scott, leaned down beside his ear, and whispered, "Bacon."

His eyes snapped open and he sniffed before he flung the covers back. They walked out to find Betsy cooking.

"I'm sorry. I tried to be quiet. You've only had about three hours."

The sorcerer rubbed his eyes and gave her a full, dimple-popping grin. "Bacon."

Marcel ran to the door and whined.

Lexi looked at the plateful of bacon, then at the dog. "Do you think he'd go on the balcony?"

The other woman guffawed. "I'm sure the people below us would be delighted."

She crouched beside the puppy. "I'll take you after breakfast."

The two friends sat at the dining table, ready to tuck into bacon, eggs, and biscuits. Scott tore a piece of bacon in half and gave it to Marcel.

"I made some for him too. I'll get his bowl." Betsy picked her apartment key up from the counter and headed across the hall.

Thirty seconds later, she returned, her expression anxious. "I think something's wrong."

The others stood quickly and hurried across the hall. The older woman remained at the back and pulled the door almost closed to stop Marcel from following.

Lexi put her head in. "Dick?"

Betsy peeked around Scott. "He's not there. I looked in all the rooms."

She nodded acknowledgment, passed the dining table, and stood with her hands on the back of the couch as she stared at the upturned bowl and the popcorn spread across the floor. "It looks like there might have been a struggle. Even if there wasn't, Dick's a neat freak. There's no way he'd leave it like this."

They turned at a shuffling sound. Betsy hadn't closed the other apartment door properly and Marcel had managed to work it open with his nose. He raced down the hallway.

Scott ran after him. "No!" He vanished and reappeared ahead of the puppy to block his way down the stairs.

The two women raced from the apartment after them. Instead of trying to run down the stairs, however, the dog spun and moved up. Lexi found him at the door to the roof where he scratched and whined. She remembered the popcorn on the stairs and looked at Scott while she drew her short-sword. When she was armed, she nodded for her friend to release the lock.

They stepped out into the morning sunlight and stopped in shock. Dick was hogtied with heavy chains and lay on the roof between a folded sun lounger and an AC unit. Marcel bounded to him and licked his face but he was out cold. Scott spoke a word and the chains shattered. He lifted the man in his arms. "I'll take him downstairs," he said before they both disappeared.

"Oh!" Betsy jumped. Marcel ran in circles and scratched at the roof where Dick had been, then lifted his leg and peed against the door before he bolted down the stairs.

The older woman turned to Lexi. "Can you disappear like that?"

She rolled her eyes. "No, we have to go the long way."

Scott had placed Dick on the couch in his apartment when the women entered. "Where are his blood bags?"

Betsy went to the fridge, then returned to Scott's side. "He uses these tubes."

The sorcerer took the bag and tube from her. "Doesn't this gross you out?"

The woman smiled. "I prefer a good chardonnay." She stroked the vampire's hair. "Will he be all right?"

"He hasn't desiccated so he's still with us. That's all I can tell you at the moment." He pierced the opening of the bag with the tube and fed it into Dick's mouth. He gave the bag a slight squeeze. They watched anxiously and after a few moments, he swallowed.

Lexi stood behind the couch while her friend hovered and squeezed the blood patiently into his mouth until his eyes fluttered open. Betsy crouched closer to him and put her hand on Dick's shoulder. "I think he's trying to speak."

Scott pulled the tube from his lips and they both leaned closer to listen.

The vampire put his hand over Betsy's. "Could you ask Lexi to stop licking my feet?"

They looked at Marcel, who stood on his hind legs with his paws on the arm of the couch, licking his feet.

Lexi rolled her eyes and went to pick the dog up but he dodged her and started on the popcorn strewn on the floor. "What happened to Mike?"

"Mike? Oh, Peter." Dick sighed. "I think they killed him." He sat stiffly. "I intend to obliterate them."

Betsy squeezed his hand and left the room.

He checked his watch, then looked around the room. "They took my shoes but not my watch?" Baffled, he shook his head.

She walked to the couch and tapped Dick's feet. He shifted them to the floor and she sat. "Who were they?"

"They mentioned someone called Lorenzo. I don't know who that is yet. They filled Peter with drugs without him knowing. I can't believe the poor man's gone and it's my fault."

Lexi frowned. "You seem to have grown attached to him remarkably quickly. How is it your fault?"

"Do you know about the exchange?"

She raised her eyebrow. "You mean the illegal blood exchange?"

The vampire stood. "Oh, don't get your panties in a twist. Remember, you're only pretending to be Kindred. The blood exchange is considered a great honor. Offering one is tantamount to adoption. If anything—by which I mean death—

happens to the donor while they have vampire blood in them, they will be reborn." He checked the time again. "I need to get changed." He walked into the bedroom.

Confused, she continued to speak to him from outside the room. "So, you did or didn't offer this to Peter?"

"I didn't. Honestly, at first, I thought he was a dud. Then it transpired he's a fan of my movies. Such a charming, well-educated young man." He returned in a dark-red velvet dressing gown.

"Which explains this." She picked the DVD case up from the table.

Betsy entered the room with a margarita. "Ah! One of my absolute favorite movies."

"But I die at the end of it. Why is it everyone's favorite?" He looked at the glass. "Isn't it a little early for that?"

"It's for you. I thought you might need it." She held the glass out.

He took it, held her hand, and kissed it. "Betsy darling, I will love you until I die…again."

She blushed.

He straightened and held a finger in the air, tilted his head, and listened. "They're back." Before anyone could ask who he meant, he was gone.

Lexi rolled her eyes and followed.

CHAPTER NINE

"Lorenzo told us to lock him up here and stay away."

"He doesn't need to know we came back."

"What's the point in going out there to clean the dust up? It's probably blown away."

"Vamp dust has a street value."

"People snort that shit?"

"Not like that. The voodoo stores might buy it."

"It's the big key. Do you want me to do it?"

"No, it isn't locked. Who was supposed to lock it last night?"

"Charlie." The voice responded a little too quickly and noticeably higher in pitch.

"Idiot."

"Well, the vacuum cleaner makes sense now."

"Time to suck up a nice little profit."

The two men stepped through the door onto the roof of the apartment building and looked around.

"It looks different in the day. I don't remember the sun lounger over there or the robe."

They walked across the roof.

"I don't see any dust. Maybe the wind blew it—"

The door slammed shut and the men spun to face Dick, who held a margarita and wore nothing but a tiny pair of Versace baroque briefs. "Gentlemen, let's talk."

The skinny guy dropped the vacuum cleaner, ran to the edge of the roof, and jumped. He screamed briefly.

The vampire stared after him before he turned to the remaining man. "But there are balconies at the front. Why on earth did he run to the back of the building?" He shrugged.

The stocky guy moved to draw a gun.

He closed the space between them in a second, grasped him by the throat, and held him several inches off the roof by the time the gun was in his hand and free of his pocket. "Let's talk about Lorenzo."

"He said you were a vamp. He'll kill me if I talk."

"You don't seem to have fully grasped your current situation. Let me help you with that." He lowered his captive, pulled his face close, and allowed his vampire teeth to descend inches from the man's eyes.

The gun clattered onto the rooftop.

"But it's daylight. I… What? We were only doing what we were told to." His voice had climbed several octaves as the toe of his boots scraped the surface of the roof.

Dick lifted him higher. "You poisoned Peter to poison me."

The man squeaked a terrified protest. "That's what Lorenzo told us to do."

He lowered him to stand on the roof but kept his hand about the man's throat. "And Lorenzo is?"

"He leads one of the clans."

The vampire frowned in thought. "I've never heard of him."

"He took over a few years ago from Giovanni."

"I liked Giovanni." He sighed. "Where is Peter?"

"We…" The man seemed to feel the need to rethink his answer. "Lorenzo told us to throw him in a dumpster. We… Lorenzo gave him enough of that stuff to—"

"Fell an ox. I heard." He tightened his hold on the man's windpipe. "It's very difficult, these days, to find an actual fan of my work, and you killed him. I have to say, I'm very upset. And where are my Christian Louboutins?"

"That's Lorenzo's…thing. He asks…for the…shoes." The man's face purpled slightly, and his breathing was shallow and gasping around the obstruction.

Lexi stepped out from where she had watched.

The captive beat a fist against the vampire's arm and pointed behind him.

Dick released his hold fractionally.

"He was going to kill me." The man stared beseechingly at her.

With a withering smile, he hoisted him again. "What do you mean, 'was?'"

"You can't kill me in front of Kindred," the man protested and kicked wildly. "They won't let you."

She leaned against the door. "Well…no, actually, I'm okay with it. Maybe you should tell him where his number-one fan is."

"In a dumpster on Conti Street—where they're fixing the old hotel up."

Lexi had taken a little knife out and cleaned her nails with it. "And why does Lorenzo want my friend here dead?"

"I don't know. He only told us to do it, not why." His face faded from purple hues to a bright red.

Dick dropped him on the roof and turned to her, about to speak. The guy scrambled to his feet and ran in the opposite direction to the one his friend had taken, straight off the building, and screamed.

She looked after him. "Why didn't he jump off the front where the balconies are?"

The vampire shrugged. "I think I might have somehow given him the impression the front of the building was that way. Did Scott catch the first one?"

The sorcerer came through the door. "He landed on our

balcony. Betsy almost had a heart attack. I sent him to sleep. Did you get what you needed from the other one?" Scott looked around for the second man, then shrugged. "If you're done here, I'll go get rid of him." He disappeared.

"Don't you think it might be best to leave Peter where he is?" Lexi wandered to the back of the building and looked down with a grimace. "That guy won't get up again."

Dick took a sip of his cocktail. "I owe it to the young man to find him and return him to his family."

"Excuse me?"

"Also, whilst I didn't offer an exchange, if he was drinking with Lorenzo or one of his clan, it's quite possible he was given vampire blood before coming to me."

"You're telling me it's still possible that Peter could turn?"

"Honestly, I doubt it. I don't think he was lying to me and he didn't seem used to socializing with us. If he were, he wouldn't have offered himself to the sanguinaires. The clans prefer to keep their supplies to themselves. They take traceability in the supply chain very seriously. But if he did exchange with another vampire, we don't want him to wake up hungry in the middle of a populated area tonight. That could be bad."

"I can see that." Lexi looked at her watch. "It's still early. I might be able to get over there before the city gets going."

Dick marched toward the door, but she put a hand out. "Where do you think you're going?"

"I thought we—"

"There is no we. You need to keep a low profile. Walking through the French Quarter in daylight wearing nothing but..." She squinted at him and all but shuddered. "Wearing really tiny briefs won't help."

"These briefs were three hundred dollars. They should be seen." He sighed. "Fine, I'll get dressed, but I'm coming."

He vanished, and in the time it took her to descend one floor, he was waiting in jeans and a hoodie.

Lexi raised her eyebrows. "You own a hoodie?"

"It's Peter's."

As she approached the apartment door, it opened and the other thug walked out. "Morning." He smiled and nodded at her. Dick turned his back discreetly until the man had rounded the corner and was halfway down the stairs.

Scott followed him out of the apartment and stopped beside her. "He's going to visit his mother in Natchez. He hasn't been the best son, so he's going to apologize."

They arrived at the tall dumpster. Lexi looked at Dick and waited.

He gazed around the quiet streets before he fixed her with a wide-eyed look. "I'm not getting in there."

"He's your friend."

"But…you owe me a dumpster from Chicago."

She rolled her eyes and turned to Scott.

He immediately took a step back. "Don't even look at me. Turn those eyeballs away."

"Oh, for God's sake. Give me a lift up." She stepped into his interlocked hands and climbed onto the edge. "I can't see him."

"Maybe he slipped beneath the top layer of slime and filth," Dick suggested.

Unimpressed, she stared at him with distaste. "There are rats and roaches in there."

"And a potential killing machine." he reminded her.

With an exasperated sigh, she dropped in. She lifted sheets of drywall and kicked roaches off her boot. "It stinks in here." She dropped the remnants of a door. "Dick, he's not in here."

"Dick's not here," Scott called in response.

"Where is he?"

The sorcerer's voice grew quieter as he continued to speak to her with his back turned. "He's across the street with a guy—oh, wait. It's Peter."

"What?" Lexi heaved herself up and glowered at where Dick talked to a man who was crouched on a doorstep. She scrambled out, dropped to the ground, and scraped something off her boot before she marched across the street.

Peter shielded his eyes and squinted at the vampire. "Bus delit."

Dick crouched beside him. "What?"

"S'dayl–" the man slurred and lowered his head.

He slapped his cheek. "What are you trying to say, Peter?"

Peter straightened a little, stretched a trembling hand, and stroked Dick's cheek. "S'okay." He leaned forward and pulled the hood up to cover the vampire's head.

"He's protecting me from the sun." He sighed and smiled, leaned in, and spoke slowly to the other man. "I'll explain everything later, but we'll take care of you first. What on earth is that awful smell?" He turned quickly. "Ah! Lexi. You're back."

She scowled at him.

He put a hand up. "Don't act like you didn't deserve that. You were in there for less than a minute. I was in that dumpster in Chicago all night with a broken neck."

Lexi gritted her teeth and looked at Peter. "How's he doing? He doesn't look dead."

"Pie-eyed, but no, not dead."

She shook her head. "How did the drugs not kill him?"

"Pfft! Do Roofies for fuuuun." The man giggled.

Dick raised an eyebrow. "Apparently, he's built up something of a resistance." He looked at Scott. "Can you do something?"

The sorcerer shook his head. "I think we should get him to the hospital. I can heal people, but I need to know what's going on with them. I haven't a clue what those drugs might have done to him."

The vampire stooped to pick the drugged man up.

Peter caught his hand and pulled it to his cheek. "Don' go, Johnny, don' go," he mumbled and burst into tears.

"There, there." Dick patted his back and glanced at Scott.

The young man retrieved his cell. "I'll call a cab."

Dick stood with the nurse. "I don't know how many. I wasn't there. I found him on a street corner."

"But you're willing to pay for his treatment." The nurse raised an eyebrow.

He plucked the forms from her hand. "He's someone's son. Wouldn't anyone with the means do the same?"

She regarded him with suspicion. "Quite frankly, Mr. Levine, no."

"Well then, thank goodness I'm not simply anyone." He ignored the pen he was offered and instead, drew his Mont Blanc special edition pen from the shirt pocket beneath his hoodie.

Lexi rolled her eyes and turned to Scott. She took a slip of paper from her pocket. "Let's visit Amy."

They took the stairs to the next floor and found the psych ward.

The police officer outside the hospital room slipped quietly into unconsciousness, oblivious to the two friends entering the room.

Amy lay cuffed to the bed and stared at the ceiling.

Lexi spoke as she entered. "Hi, Amy, we'd like to ask you some questions if that's okay."

The girl kept her gaze fixed on the ceiling. "I heard them say they know who did it. They'll let me go after a psych evaluation."

Lexi moved to the chair beside the bed. "Can you tell me what happened?"

"I don't know. I woke up and—" Amy closed her eyes and

tears ran from the corner of her eyes into her hair. "It was horrible."

She lowered her voice when she asked the next question. "When we found you, the machete was in your hand. Do you remember picking it up?"

"I woke up on the couch. I thought someone was there. It felt like someone was close by. I grabbed it and hid. I don't remember anything else. Everything was fine. We were only doing some...I don't know, ritual stuff."

Scott asked, "What was the ritual?"

"Jamal wanted to speak to Marie Laveau." The girl blinked and tears streamed from her eyes.

The two friends shared a look.

Scott leaned against the wall and folded his arms. "Using the ring you stole from the museum."

Amy blushed and she nodded.

Lexi leaned forward. "Where is it now?"

She shrugged and rattled the bracelet cuffed to the bed's railing. "When I woke up, I wasn't wearing it. They said a woman came in and killed Jamal. Maybe she stole it."

Scott muttered, "Sleep." Amy closed her eyes.

"Excuse me, what are you doing in here?"

James from Thought and Memory, the witchcraft store, stood in the doorway. He wore scrubs.

He raised an eyebrow. "Oh, it's you."

She blinked. "I thought you worked in the witchcraft store."

James continued into the room. "Sam and I help out when we can. She won't leave the place."

Lexi moved away from the bed. "Why do you want her to leave?"

The man moved to the notes and checked them. He flicked a glance at Lexi. "You haven't noticed? Everyone's getting out. With all this shit going down with the vampires. Do you honestly think we haven't seen what's been going on? You look away while your pals make moves. I'm amazed you all weren't away for longer."

She pinched the bridge of her nose. "I don't understand this."

"You need to leave. The doctor's coming to assess her." James spun on his heel and marched down the hallway.

"What the hell was that about?" she asked.

Scott shrugged.

Back in the ER, they found Dick seated in a bay next to Peter's bed.

The sorcerer took the chart from the end of the bed. "How's he looking?"

"They've pumped his stomach and he's on saline and electrolytes. They'll test his liver and kidneys."

Scott replaced the chart and placed his hand on the patient's stomach. "His kidneys are fine. His liver's not great and he needs to hold off on the booze and recreational drugs. I think he'll be out of here in twenty-four to forty-eight hours."

Lexi patted the vampire's shoulder. "Hey, the museum case is solved."

Dick held his gaze on the patient. "Oh, that's right. Amy stole the ring. I realized that last night."

She stood with her mouth agape.

"I've been a little busy." He gestured a hand in Peter's direction.

"I've just seen Anne Bird's son. He seems to think Kindred are allowing one vampire clan to dominate the city."

He straightened. "Oh, yes. Betsy and I spoke to an old shifter friend of mine yesterday morning. She thinks Kindred were behind Palm Springs and that they left to allow this little war to happen. But we know that's not true."

Lexi thought about it as she chewed the inside of her cheek. "They do seem to be taking their time to get back here."

They sat with Peter for a couple of hours until his results came back and confirmed Scott's assessment.

She rose. "I need to find Broullard. Will you stay here?"

"No." Dick smiled an unattractive smile "I need to get out of sight."

"I don't think any other vamps will see you out in the daylight."

"Oh, I'll visit them soon enough." He stood and kissed the now sleeping Peter on his forehead.

They headed out of the hospital and waited for a cab.

The vampire took sunglasses from his pocket and slid them onto his face. "What will you tell the detective?"

"He'll need to know Amy killed Jamal while she was possessed by this Marie Laveau woman."

He shook his head. "That makes no sense. I honestly can't see it. Marie Laveau was beloved and known for her kindness and deep religious convictions. What could have happened to her spirit to make her hack someone up like that?"

When the cab pulled up at the apartment block, Lexi looked up and scowled when she saw Betsy wasn't alone on the balcony. Agatha was with her. She glanced at Scott. "This can't be good."

When they entered, Agatha made eye contact with the sorcerer.

She watched the exchange. "Another one. Well, at least I won't have to hunt the detective."

They followed the girl to Decatur Street.

The two friends waited patiently with the crowd at the end of the alley beyond the cordon until Broullard noticed them. He stepped out from behind the tape and signaled them to walk with him. "You're late."

They joined a line for coffee.

"We were at the hospital." Scott pulled a ten-dollar bill from his pocket.

Broullard turned. "Did you leave with Amy?"

Lexi narrowed her eyes. "No. We spoke to her. She was waiting for a psych evaluation. Why?"

He moved to the front of the line. "Can I get three flat whites, please?" He turned to the others and motioned to Scott to put his money away. "I've just had a call from the station. The doctor discharged her to the care of her parents, but when they arrived, she'd already left. Admittedly, she's no longer a suspect and not much of a witness. They've been to the apartment and she's not there either. It looks like this one's ours after all. It seems to be a case of simply bat-shit crazy."

Her gaze flicked to the sorcerer before it returned to Broullard. "That might not be the case."

He paid for the coffee and they walked to the end of the counter. With a sigh, he glanced around to make sure they wouldn't be overheard. "Go on."

Lexi began to pick up sachets of sugar. "Are you aware of the break-in at the Museum of Death?"

"Yes, I heard about it." He stared at her coffee. "What happened to *'pure, white and deadly?'*"

Lexi looked at her drink, utterly clueless about what he meant. "It was Amy. She stole Marie Laveau's ring to try to communicate with her spirit. We think she was possessed and went to town on Jamal. Cora found the ring when she went in to clean-slash-burgle the apartment. She went home, put it on, and took her husband's head off."

They took their drinks and returned to the crime scene.

Broullard blew on his coffee. "I've seen some weird shit in my time, but from the way people speak about Marie Laveau, there's simply no way she would be that kind of spirit."

"I agree."

Lexi startled and spun quickly. "Joseph, I swear—"

Joseph traced the patterns on his staff idly with his finger and looked at her. "I think it's time for you to return to the museum."

The cop nodded. "I've never known you to be wrong, Joseph." He turned to her. "Do you want to check this one before you go?"

She turned to him. "What's missing this time?"

"Au contraire, a piece of lost property has appeared." Broullard lifted the tape for her but dropped it in front of Scott. She passed her coffee to her friend.

They walked up the narrow alley and her nose twitched at the smell of garbage and rat piss. The body of a man lay on the ground. The first thing she observed was the shiny shoes. Then she noticed a burn hole in his pants. Her gaze trailed to his face. It wasn't one she had expected to see.

Broullard lifted the blood-soaked collar to show large, industrial staples. "This is Ambrose. Well, it's his head…stapled to an unknown's body."

Lexi looked at him, a little startled. "It's the shoeshine extortion guy."

He took a notepad and pen out. "You'll have to narrow that down."

"He has a gold tooth and hangs with a shorter guy. We passed him on Decatur near Jackson Square. Scott could probably tell you his name."

"Tyrone?" he asked. She nodded. "Well, now we're looking for Tyrone's head and I'm thinking of retiring."

CHAPTER TEN

Agatha walked along the street, thinking about the Kindred lady and how she smelled strange. She couldn't put her finger on what was strange about her. And why wasn't she staying at the usual Kindred place? What was that about? It wasn't a problem, obviously. She had her weird scent and could track her with an hours' old trail.

She smiled. *If this is how good I am now, imagine how awesome I'll be when I shift. It'll be soon, I'm sure.*

As she passed a gate, she detected an unusual odor. The girl stopped, turned her head and sniffed, and peered up the narrow corridor along the side of the big house. The smell was out of place, and she'd never seen this gate open before. She crept quietly along the side of the building and tried to remember where she'd encountered the scent before. Was it food? The door of the building stood ajar and brought her closer to identifying the smell. She pressed her face to the sliver of open doorway. It swung in about a foot and stopped. She sniffed again.

What is it?

With one tentative step after another, Agatha entered the house.

She was four or five steps in when finally, it hit her what the smell was.

Blood.

Instinctively, she spun toward the door, but a woman stood in her way with a knife in one hand and a man's head in the other. Agatha whirled and ran into the mansion. She entered a large white hallway dominated by a glittering chandelier. When she reached the front doors, she twisted one handle, then the next, but it was no use. The door was locked and soft footsteps approached from behind.

She bolted to the right and flew up a wide, curved staircase as fast as her young legs would take her.

At the next level, she turned. The woman was no longer behind her. She took her shoes off to quieten the sound and ran along another hallway to the door at the end. Relieved, she reached for the handle but stopped. The smell drifted to her again. Her pursuer was on the other side of the door. She could feel it. Her mind raced and when she glanced out the window beside her, she realized she was at the back of the house. This door would lead to the back stairway used by servants or slaves. The mansion was old.

Agatha backed away quietly, returned to the curved staircase, and continued up. She tried several rooms but most of them were empty and she could find nowhere to hide. Finally, she entered what appeared to be a large sewing room with a big table in the center. A giant pair of scissors rested on top of a pile of fabric. A sewing machine stood on a smaller table near the window beside a mannequin, and rolls of fabric leaned against a wall.

She was about to pick the scissors up when something caught her eye. Her heart thudding, she ran around the table to the window and halted at the sight of a young blonde woman on the floor. Her hands were tied and although she seemed to be awake, she couldn't get any response from her. The window was locked and there weren't enough rolls of fabric to hide behind. There were closets in this room, but the woman would surely look in closets.

A little desperate now, she glanced down. Beneath the closets were small cupboards with two sliding doors—the kind you might put shoes in or that adults might overlook. She slid a door open and peered inside. It didn't appear to be in use so she scrambled into the small space and slid the door closed with her foot. She opened the door near her face the tiniest of fractions to allow her a glimpse into the room. The woman on the floor was mostly out of view. Her nose twitched.

Lord, it's dusty in here!

In the silence, she wished she could shift. If she could, she'd be able to rip the woman's throat out. She'd heard of children shifting before their time, usually brought on by a stressful situation. Maybe this situation counted as stressful.

I'd better not shift in this tiny space. I'll break my neck.

The door to the room opened. The woman entered, swinging the head in her hand. Agatha closed her eyes.

"We have a guest." The woman seemed to be speaking to the blonde. The girl looked through the sliver and willed herself to not close her eyes. "We'll have a little fun." She walked to the mannequin, pulled its head up and dropped it onto the floor, then replaced it with the head in her hand and squashed it onto the body. "There."

The youngster swallowed a sob and closed her eyes again. The woman came closer and the closet door above her opened, then closed, followed by another.

The feet turned away, walked across the room, and out. The door clicked closed and Agatha released a breath.

Then, without warning, she sneezed.

Horrified, she held her breath and waited to see if the woman had heard.

CHAPTER ELEVEN

Lexi and Scott entered the Museum of Death. He shivered and she felt his disquiet.

The same man they'd seen on the night of the break-in was behind the cash register with his back to her.

She walked to the counter. "I heard the boss is back."

The guy turned. "You just missed him. He's freaking out about the mix-up."

"The mix-up?"

"You don't know?" He led them to the back of the building. The cabinet had been replaced and she crossed to it quickly. Marie Laveau's picture was still in place but now, beneath it, was a label stating, *Marie Laveau's ring.* Beside it rested a shiny ring with a blue stone.

Her eyes wandered to the picture of a stern-looking woman beside Marie's picture and read the label in front of the picture, *Marie Delphine LaLaurie's ring.* There was a space where the ring should be.

"Exactly." He released an exasperated breath.

Lexi raised an eyebrow. "Am I to assume she stole the wrong ring?"

"It looks that way. We need to get the other one back and without delay, obviously. Here's a picture of the ring we're looking for."

She looked at the image and the woman's photograph again. She wasn't about to admit that she didn't know who she was either. "Obviously. Well, no time like the present."

They stepped outside and Scott shook himself as if to loosen anything that might have clung to him. "I hope I never have to go back in there again."

"Stop. Please—wait," a voice called.

They turned to see a couple walking hurriedly toward them.

The woman held a toddler in her arms. "Have you seen her? We've looked everywhere."

Lexi blinked. "I'm sorry?"

"Aggie. She was supposed to find you and take you to the detective, then come straight home."

She stepped closer to respond, but the woman stepped back.

Why the hell are these people so afraid of Kindred?

"She delivered us to Broullard maybe an hour and a half ago. I didn't see her after that."

The man felt in his pocket and pulled a little doll out. "She always comes back. This is very unusual. I'm worried. Can you find her for us? We don't want to bother you—"

"It's fine. That's what we're here for." Scott attempted to take the doll, but the man jerked his arm away.

His eyes narrowed and he watched the sorcerer suspiciously. "Who are you?"

Lexi interjected before her friend could share his name. "He's with me. I'm training him." *What the hell. It worked with Broullard.*

After a moment, the man passed the doll to Scott. The sorcerer muttered a few words and began to walk.

Agatha's parents followed but remained a short distance behind as though they didn't want to be seen with them. That was fine with Lexi.

At her signal, her friend created a barrier around them.

He nodded to confirm it was safe to speak and she wasted no time. "Do you any idea who Marie Darlene—"

"Marie Delphine LaLaurie," he interrupted.

"Great, you know her."

"No, I merely have a better memory than a goldfish—or you."

Lexi sighed. "We need to know who she is. Can you look it up?"

She took the doll from him and felt its pull as it sought its owner.

Scott scrolled through his cell. "Okay, Marie Delphine LaLaurie. Born 1787, died 1849… Oh. Oh, dear. As soon as we've found Agatha, we need to make finding that ring our number one priority."

When she glanced at him, his face was pale. "You will have to give me more information than that, you know."

His gaze remained fixed ahead. "A rich lady of the city who tortured, experimented on, and butchered her slaves."

"Slaves! Jamal, Ambrose, and Tyrone were all African American."

"Exactly."

Lexi halted and turned to him. "So we have the spirit of a racist psychopath running around the city."

He sighed.

"Well, fuck!" She scratched her head and scowled.

Scott continued to read. "There's some sick stuff in here, but it says most of it is probably only urban myths."

"You saw what she did to Jamal. Do you think what she did was mythical?"

They increased their speed.

"We must have walked ten blocks. Where the hell is she?"

The doll tugged. "Okay, we're turning here." Lexi looked back. Agatha's parents were still about twenty paces behind them.

Her friend was still reading. "It says here that she's buried in St. Louis Cemetery Number One. Oh, or Paris."

They crossed Bourbon Street with its busy bars and restaurants and continued.

She tried to think what their next move should be. "Where did she live while she was here? Could the building still be standing?"

"Looking… A big mansion. The LaLaurie mansion. It's a nice-looking place. They say it's haunted."

Lexi shook the doll. "No shit. Wait, it's stopped pulling." She looked around for signs of Agatha.

Scott looked up from his screen. "Lexi?"

"What is it?"

He held the cellphone up so she could see. It showed a picture of the LaLaurie mansion. When he lowered his arm, she stared at the same building directly in front of her.

They turned to Agatha's parents. The horror on their faces confirmed that they knew exactly where they were.

As she returned the doll to the girl's stricken mother, her husband bolted across the street and through the open side gate.

"Wait." Scott ran after him.

Lexi looked at her scar, which was empty again. She turned to follow but a flicker of movement drew her attention. Joseph had appeared—from thin air, as usual—and pointed up. Her gaze followed and she muttered an expletive when a third-story window shattered and a sheet of material rolled from it. Agatha climbed out after it.

Her mother gasped. Lexi glanced at the woman, who put her hand to her mouth. Her eyes flashed from brown to gold and back to brown and she obviously fought the urge to shift. She stood on a public street and would incur a Kindred death sentence if she shifted. Fortunately, she held her son so would resist the instinct.

Agatha started to climb down the fabric but had only

managed to descend about a foot from the window ledge when Cora appeared at the window. She thrust her hand out holding a knife, the ring clearly visible. With a cruel smile, she sliced the tenuous lifeline. It tore the rest of the way and the child fell.

Her mother screamed.

"No!" Lexi raced forward from the opposite corner with her arms out as though she might catch her, but she was too far away.

A moment later, she landed on her knees with the weight of the twelve-year-old girl who had translocated now in her arms. She huffed at the impact and her elbows and knees scraped painfully. The girl sat and threw her arms around her. A moment later, she saw her mother, scrambled to her feet, and ran to her.

Lexi tried to stand but fell back. The translocation had taken everything, even the strength in her muscles. But Scott had run into a building with a psychopath waiting. She wasn't about to let him die. Joseph extended his hand to her. She initially thought he was offering to pull her up, but he slipped something into her hand.

A little bemused, she looked into her open palm at a stone with sigils painted onto it.

"This has power," he said.

She looked up to ask what kind of power but of course, he was gone.

Come on then, power stone. Help me get off my ass.

Lexi tried to stand again, and as she wobbled, arms came around her and raised her to her feet. Energy pulsed into her muscles and she turned to Anne Bird and her daughter Sam.

She nodded her thanks to them and ran through the gate and into the house. Inside, there was blood on the floor. She yanked her katana out and glanced at her scar. Scott's magic was completely drained and she couldn't understand how she had been able to use it to save Agatha. He still wasn't close enough to replenish it.

You're a disappointment, she told the stone in her left hand, shook it, and flipped it in the air.

Her senses alert, she crept through the house and her soft-soled boots made no sound on the tiled floor.

When she rounded the staircase to the second floor, she found Tyrone's head on a plinth. She paused to listen for any indication of where Scott might be. With the choice of a long hallway or the stairs to the next story, she looked from one to the other. When she returned her gaze to the hallway, a black wolf stared at her. Agatha's dad, obviously, and that made her decision easy. The wolf had cleared that level. She nodded and moved to the stairs. Before she headed up, she looked at him and whispered, "She's okay. She's out front."

Lexi reached the next level and immediately saw Scott walk out of a room ahead of her. He jumped at the sight of her and she smirked and rolled her eyes. After a less than polite hand gesture, he pointed to the opposite hallway to indicate that she should check it. He turned right and made his way to the end of the hallway. As he opened the door, Lexi stopped and turned. He entered a bright, sunny room where Amy sat in the middle of the floor.

What the hell is she doing here?

Scott hurried to the girl, crouched beside her, and checked her vitals. Even from this distance, it was obvious that she was catatonic again.

A shape broke away from the shadows and approached him from behind. It was Cora, and she held the knife. Lexi broke into a run and slid her hand into her pocket to pull out a gun or throwing knife.

Cora's brainwashed. I can't kill her for that.

She felt the weight of the stone in her other hand. *This will do.* It would distract her for the seconds she needed. She threw the stone at the woman and it was a perfect shot and caught her squarely in the temple.

What she hadn't anticipated was the explosion. It wasn't loud, but a bright flash followed immediately by a wet whoosh left Scott, Amy, the room, and part of the hallway covered in a coat of red.

Lexi, who had barely reached the entrance, skidded to a halt in the blood. Her jaw hung open in shock at the devastating transformation of the view before her. She shook her head several times while wet gore dripped from the ceiling. Cora had been completely obliterated.

"Wh…wh…wh." Scott finally gave up.

His body had protected Amy from the worst of it although, as she had suspected, the girl had zoned out again. *Small mercies.* The sorcerer stood holding his arms away from his body. "This is so bad."

Rivulets of red ran from his hair into a gap in the back of his collar. He turned slowly and stared at her.

"It's not my fault. It was the stone—I didn't know it would do that." She stopped speaking under the intensity of his withering stare.

"Why is it always me?" Scott's voice was a squeak.

Lexi giggled. It was involuntary and she clamped her jaw until the compulsion left her. "Can't you whoosh it somewhere else like you did in Palm Springs?"

He sighed. "It's different magic. I have no fucking idea what you did."

"She was coming up behind you with a blade but I was trying to avoid killing her."

"That went well," he snipped.

She stared around the red room. "Can you see the ring?"

"Are you looking at this room?" He waved his hand wildly. "She and everything on her is liquid. It must have been on her but there's no way to find it now." He sighed and looked at the catatonic girl. "Let's take Amy to the apartment. We can clean her up and try to unfuck her brain before her parents see her."

The sorcerer incanted a glamor so he and Amy could walk

through New Orleans without horrifying the citizens. They stepped onto the street.

Agatha came running and put her arms around Lexi. "Are you okay?" She looked at Scott. "You smell bad."

Lexi waved her hand in front of her face. "Phew! I know—boys, right?"

The youngster laughed while she pretended to be oblivious to Scott's scowl.

The parents headed away with their daughter while the two friends made their way to the apartment with Amy.

The girl gazed fixedly ahead and required nothing more than his hand on her back to direct her. Within a few blocks, they were at the apartments, where Betsy and Lexi removed Amy's blood-soaked clothes and Scott threw them into the washer with his own. The young woman simply stood staring into who knew what while they wrapped her in Betsy's gown. The two women left her there, still in a daze, and stepped into the bathroom.

Betsy washed the blood from her hands. "Will Scott be able to bring her out of this?"

Lexi directed her to a towel before washing her hands. "Possibly. I think we should let her rest while her clothes are cleaned, then Broullard can take her. It's a good thing Scott took most of that. Otherwise, we'd be washing it out of her hair."

The other woman frowned. "How will we encourage her to rest? Could we poke her to topple her onto the bed?"

She threw the towel into the bath. "I think you've spent way too much time with Dick."

They entered the bedroom to find Amy curled in the bed with her eyes closed.

"I'll be honest, that was easier than I expected." She looked at Betsy. "I need to speak to Scott."

"That's fine. Leave her with me. I'll read my book and stay close."

They walked up the hall and the older woman settled into an armchair while she headed across to the other apartment.

Dick passed her a coffee as she entered. "All quiet?"

"Yes. Betsy's reading and Amy's sleeping. How's Scott?" She blew on her drink before she took a sip.

"I'm here and I'm fine." He walked into the room in shorts with his blond hair in damp waves.

Lexi sniffed and looked toward the kitchen. "What's that smell?"

"I incinerated my clothes." He took a mug from Dick.

"I'm sorry about the…I don't even know what to call that." She grimaced.

"Deconstruction?" the vampire suggested helpfully.

"It's as good a word as any." Scott shrugged.

She studied him anxiously. *He looks traumatized.*

The vampire sat and Marcel jumped into his lap. He looked at her. "I guess you're back on track with your investigation into the photograph. I'll pay a visit to this Lorenzo chap and see if we can have a heart-to-heart about his manners."

"I'll come and watch your back. Scott, I think you should rest."

The sorcerer nodded. He scrolled and tapped on his cell while he extended his arm across the counter to her. She slid her hand into his to refill the magical energy.

Dick smirked at them. "A picture of domestic bliss."

They both flipped him the bird.

The vampire put Marcel onto the floor and went to the door. "I'll get ready, then."

After a few minutes, she finished her coffee and thumped Scott's shoulder. "Get some rest."

Scott watched as Lexi left the apartment. He returned his gaze to his cell and typed.

I know where that is. I can meet you there in twenty minutes.

Quickly, he dressed, looked in on Betsy, and headed out of the building and down the street. Moments later, he turned left onto Bourbon street and walked several blocks until he reached a small eatery. He looked at the sign—Nola Po'boys—and entered. The unassuming establishment was rumored to sell some of the best local dishes in New Orleans. He ordered a catfish po'boy to go, put his bag down, and took a seat in a booth opposite an unhealthy looking man who fidgeted with a package. "Is this it?"

The man nodded but made no other movement.

He waited for a response before he prompted, "Can I see it?"

After a furtive glance around the room, his companion slid the package across the table. Scott looked inside and smiled. He squeezed the contents in his hand and his smile broadened. He passed some folded notes across the table. "That'll do nicely."

The stranger snaked his hand out and the money was gone. He stood and left without a backward glance.

The sorcerer glanced around, sure that no one was watching. He took the item from its packaging and pushed it into his bag— or more precisely, into a specific room in his dimensional pocket. The server brought his po'boy and he left to walk to the apartment.

CHAPTER TWELVE

The women spoke in hushed tones as they retreated along the hallway. The apartment door opened and closed.

Marie Delphine LaLaurie opened her eyes.

She raised a finger to her face and slipped it into her mouth. When she removed it, she wore the ring.

Delphine had known the importance of the ring instantly. When she gazed at it through the young girl's eyes, she knew it to be hers. She remembered scrubbing dried blood from the claws around the stones after an evening's entertainment at the mansion. Her brows lowered at the thought of what had once been her stronghold. She hadn't recognized the mansion when she returned as Cora and Amy. Everything was different—everything was different *everywhere*. The only things that hadn't changed were the toys. Their screams sounded exactly as she remembered them.

With a small smile, she rolled onto her back and stretched her arms into the air. Amy's skin was pale and young. It made her recall her life before and how her skin had begun to loosen and wrinkle with age but now, it was young again. She rose from the bed and studied the slight form in the mirror.

The girl was too skinny—was she sick? She thought about some of the games she'd played in that slender body. They should have been difficult with her scrawny little arms, but she was filled with a power she'd never experienced before. Taking the boy's spine had been easy. Cora had been even stronger but she liked Amy's delicate features more. She opened the robe. The girl wasn't perfect, though. Her breasts were too small.

She touched the face and thought about the shock on it when she approached Amy outside her apartment as Cora, held a knife to her throat, and forced her to put the ring on. For a moment, she'd considered leaving the older woman in the street with the knife in her gut, but they were so pliant after she'd taken them over that it didn't hurt to keep her around.

Cora's body had been exhausted when she'd had to pursue the little girl. It had been unfortunate that she'd had to race through the house and search all the rooms, only to lose the little shit. She'd barely managed to shove the ring into Amy's mouth seconds before the blond boy came in.

Delphine turned from the mirror. She pulled the robe around her and walked along the hallway to the living room.

Almost soundless, she crept past the sleeping Betsy, walked to the kitchen, and drew a knife from the block. A thrill ran down her spine as she tested the blade. She returned to the living room and stood over Betsy, who remained asleep with a book in her lap. Until now, she had avoided looking directly at the woman before for fear she might give away that she had been aware of her surroundings. She stared at the long, lustrous, dark hair, full lips, and rounded breasts. This would be the perfect body. She would take this new body out and find new toys to play with.

Her mind made up, she aligned her finger with the other woman's—not touching, but close. In one quick movement, as she had done as Cora with Amy, she slid the ring from her finger directly onto her new body's.

Betsy's eyes jerked open and in a moment, Delphine went

from looking down at her to looking up at Amy. She smiled at the young blonde, whose face slackened as she gazed unseeingly into the distance. With a calm, unhurried motion, she stood, took the knife from the catatonic girl's hand, and led her to bed.

She left the bedroom and was walking through the apartment when the door opened.

Dick entered and greeted her with a smile. "How's Amy?"

With easy nonchalance, she picked the book up and hid the hand with the ring carefully beneath it as she settled into the chair and tucked the knife under her thigh. "I just checked on her. No change."

"I'm going to visit Lorenzo. I'll be back in time for dinner and I'll take you somewhere nice with a jazz band."

"That will be lovely." She smiled. "Have a nice time with Lorenzo."

He raised an eyebrow. "Betsy, you have a strange sense of humor."

Delphine lifted the book and felt she'd made a mistake but had gotten away with it.

Once he'd left the apartment, she headed to the bedroom to change. The tight black dress she wore was perfect and she stood before the mirror to admire it a little longer. She heard the door again.

"Betsy?" said a man's voice.

She slipped a gown on over the dress and peeked out to see the young, blond man. "Yes?"

"I'm popping out but I should only be an hour. Do you want anything?"

"No, thank you." She smiled at the sound of the door closing.

Although a little impatient, she waited ten minutes before she stepped out and closed the door quietly.

Delphine knew these streets. Things had changed, of course, but not everything.

The bar was loud and she stepped to the counter and ordered

a glass of rye whiskey. While she waited, she gazed around her. She turned to the mirror behind the bar and studied Betsy's face, pleased that it showed none of the outrage she felt.

The barman poured the drink and quoted the price.

"Let me find that for you." She smiled and opened the woman's purse.

"Make that two, please, barman. I'll get these."

She turned at the sound of the deep melodious voice and looked into the eyes of the tall handsome black man. "Why, aren't you…" Her gaze took him in, and she paused deliberately before she smiled. "Simply charming." He lifted the drinks and she followed him to a table.

He smiled. "I'm Bobby. May I ask your name, beautiful woman?"

"I'm so pleased to meet you, Robert. I'm Delphine."

"To the beautiful Delphine." He held his glass up.

With a coy smile, she held her glass up. "And to the devastatingly handsome Bobby."

They clinked glasses and drank.

The man leaned forward. "So, what do you do?"

"Do?" She was puzzled. For a moment, she wondered if he referred to her little entertainments.

"For a job," he clarified.

"Oh, I see. Well, my friend Bobby, I create sculptures—of a kind."

"Ah! An artist. Might I have seen any of your work?"

"Oh, a few pieces have been on display around the Quarter, recently. Who knows?" She laughed. "What do you…do?"

"I am in the Navy, ma'am. Speaking of which, I see some of my brothers-in-arms over there. Would you mind if I invite them to join us?"

Delphine looked at the bar and noticed two more muscular black men.

Ah! My friend Bobby is playing with me. Men. Then, now...they never really change. But I like to play too.

Betsy's face split into a huge grin. "Bobby, I would be thrilled to meet your friends."

Two other men joined them at the table.

"This is Darnell and Cole. Boys, this is Delphine. She's an artist."

Darnell sat and Cole went to get drinks. When he returned, she looked at each of them in turn.

The atmosphere had become predatory. She smiled, knowing these men were unaware of who was predator and who was prey.

"How interesting." She leaned toward Bobby. "You have the finest arms I have ever seen." She turned to Cole. "And you have the most beautiful eyes." Finally, she gazed at the third man. "You have the loveliest lips. Are you gentlemen by any chance interested in sculpture? I find myself in need of new subjects."

"We would be honored." Bobby flashed quick glances at the other men.

"Let's go to my place of residence, it's rather small—embarrassingly so—but I'm sure we could continue our conversation there in private." She couldn't wait to get them home and fulfill her plan to make the perfect man.

CHAPTER THIRTEEN

Dick showed his teeth to enter the private bar. It wasn't difficult to locate Lorenzo, who sat on a dais surrounded by half-naked women. He almost laughed. A young woman draped her arm over his and he noticed it was peppered with bite marks. He looked at the arm, then unsmilingly to her face. She stepped back.

The vampire was aware of the gazes fixed on him as he navigated the room. The small pockets of conversation around him had ceased.

He ordered a drink at the bar and turned. It wasn't necessary to shout across the room as they were vampires and his quarry would hear. He leaned lazily on the bar. "Lorenzo, can I buy you a drink?"

Lorenzo looked up as though he hadn't previously noticed him. He smiled disingenuously. "I'll have what you're having."

Dick flicked a glance at the barman. "Another, please." He smiled warmly at Lorenzo—he was an actor, after all. "Ice?"

The man flicked a hand. "As it comes."

"Rohypnol?" He raised an eyebrow.

Lorenzo smiled wider and his teeth descended. "As it comes."

The vampire took both drinks to an empty table in the middle of the room and sat. He placed the second next to the empty chair opposite him.

His quarry left the dais and appeared in the chair at vamp speed.

"I'm William. My friends call me—well, never mind. I don't think we've met."

The man's mask slipped briefly and his eyes flickered with annoyance.

Dick pretended surprise. "We have met? My bad."

Lorenzo flicked his hand in a dismissive gesture. "I was in the clan when Giovanni led it. You would have no reason to remember me."

He leaned forward. "Lorenzo, I feel there's an elephant in the room. A Peter-shaped elephant. Why on earth did you try to have me killed?"

"We run a tight ship here. I lead the largest and soon to be the only vampire clan in New Orleans. I expect visitors to present themselves within twenty-four hours of arrival. If they don't, I take it as a personal insult and their lives are forfeit." He threw his drink back. "Thank you for the drink. But your life is still forfeit." In an instant, he was on his throne and the table was surrounded by six vampires.

Dick sighed and finished his drink. "Are you sure I can't change your mind about this, Lorenzo?"

His quarry looked up with every appearance of having forgotten about him already. He looked at the vampires surrounding the table. "Why is he still here?"

The enforcers took a step forward but in the space of two seconds, three of them were headless. Their bodies thudded and began to desiccate.

The others turned in circles, looking for the threat, and Lorenzo stood as he shoved his naked donors aside.

A loud bang caught everyone's attention. Lexi had allowed

herself to become visible. She appeared at the bar and smacked her bloody katana onto the counter. "Hello, Lorenzo. I think we need to talk about your ship."

In the moment when he saw Lexi, Lorenzo's lips began to shift into a smile. This faded, however, when his brain caught up with what she had done. His jaw dropped. "But I thought Kindred—"

"You thought what?" she asked innocently.

A vampire near her rocketed toward her but froze about a foot away, paralyzed by a magical shield around her.

"Do you see what I'm talking about, Lorenzo? How is this respect?" She flicked her katana and the dead vampire dropped.

That's the last of the magic.

"Tobey!" A young human blood donor screamed and threw herself at Lexi, who punched her in the face. The girl collapsed, unconscious, beside her desiccating friend.

"This crap will stop or we'll back another clan." She walked to the door and turned to the room to point at Dick, who followed her. "And he's off-limits. Have I made myself clear?"

The vampire turned to her as they walked through the French Quarter. "So, it's true. Kindred is backing a clan?"

She looked around as she walked. "He doesn't have much of a poker face. When he saw me, his face went from joy to confusion to annoyance in a second. He definitely has a deal going with Kindred."

Dick took a handkerchief from his pocket and blotted the bloodstains on his suit. "I haven't personally read the Kindred rulebook, but I suspect cutting deals with factions isn't in it."

"Correct. Speaking of Kindred. Surely they'll be back soon. I didn't get very far in my investigation."

"No, but you took a murderer off the streets and saved a few lives." He sighed. "But you're right. I think we've outstayed our welcome here."

Lexi grimaced. "Scott will be annoyed with me. He hates it

when I put my katana in the dimensional pocket without cleaning it first. That's the problem with you vamps. I can't wipe my blade on you to get the blood off because you instantly start turning to dust, which only makes it more of a mess."

He looked at her with an eyebrow raised. "We're sorry."

She spun as a hand caught her shoulder. "Holy shit, Scott. I could have taken your head off."

The sorcerer chuckled. "Aww. It's cute you think you could do that."

"What are you doing out?" She scanned the area warily. "Did Broullard pick Amy up already?"

He made his own study of the street as they spoke. "I'm looking for Betsy. She was going to watch Amy but when I went to check on them, Amy was asleep and Betsy was nowhere in sight."

Dick looked immediately concerned. "Why didn't you do a locator spell?"

"I tried." He paused and clearly didn't want to say the next part. "She's not showing up."

"Could—" Lexi asked but couldn't complete the question.

Scott shook his head. "She's not in Fae. I called Dolores."

The vampire dragged his fingers over his scalp. "What did you use to locate her?"

The sorcerer dug in his pocket and held the object out. "Her wedding ring."

Dick took it. "She never takes it off—never."

Lexi started walking and snatched Scott's hand to refill her magic reservoir. "Okay, let's get back to the apartment. We'll see if she's returned, then we can fan out from there and cover more ground. Can Dolores join us? We shouldn't leave Amy alone."

They entered the building and found Broullard waiting outside their apartment door. "Tell me you have Amy. Her parents are going nuts."

"We have her." Scott opened the door to the front apartment and walked in. "Betsy?"

There was no response.

The cop did a double-take and stared at Dick. Clearly, he'd identified him as a vampire.

"Broullard, this is our neighbor, Dick. He's lost his friend Betsy and we're helping him locate her."

"Detective. Lexi speaks very highly of you." He shook the detective's hand, unlocked the door to his apartment, and opened it.

"She does? Well, that's great. I don't mean to be rude, but—"

"What the actual fuck?" The vampire's voice emerged as a squeak when he stepped into the apartment.

With a sigh, she waited at her door for a moment and was about to enter when Dick's raised voice made her step into the hallway again. "Young man, if you don't get out of here, I can guarantee there will be nothing left of any of you."

A man's voice responded. "I think that should be up to our lady friend."

Lexi and Broullard glanced at each other. Two men bolted from the apartment and down the hall as though the devil himself were after them. A third was shoved through the door. He turned and squared up to the vampire. The cop coughed lightly and put his hand casually on his hip to reveal the police badge. The man saw it and allowed Dick to escort him along the hall.

He turned to him. "Seriously, dude, she's kinda weird anyway."

Scott signaled to Broullard. "I'll take you to Amy." He led the detective across the hall to the other apartment where Betsy leaned on the door, twirled her hair around a finger, and winked suggestively at the young man.

She stepped aside to let them in "There's room inside for two more big ones." She smiled at the detective.

Lexi stepped into her apartment with her eyebrows almost at her hairline. *Wow!*

Dick waited at the top of the stairway for a few seconds, then returned to her apartment. He marched around the room and threw his arms up. "Sailors. Three fucking sailors. Call Dolores." He pointed toward their apartment. "She's going to Fae—tonight." He was almost hyperventilating.

She put a hand on his shoulder. "Dick, breathe. Or don't. Honestly, I don't know what's best in this situation."

Scott returned. "Betsy's helping Broullard get Amy ready. When she's dressed, I'll try to bring her out of the catatonia."

Relieved that this, at least, seemed to be close to resolution, she nodded. "When Amy and Broullard have gone, I want to do a locator spell with the key we got from Anne Bird. Let's see if I can find what it opens before Kindred gets back."

Scott inclined his head to indicate his agreement.

Dick took the ring out and put it on the table. "Why didn't the locator work with her ring?"

The young sorcerer's face went slack.

"What?" Lexi could feel a jolt of shock through their empathetic connection.

"The ring. Betsy's wearing the ring."

No one had to ask which ring. Suddenly, she was alone. Scott had disappeared and Dick had raced at vamp speed to the other apartment.

When she entered it, Scott crouched over Broullard who lay face-down with a carving knife in his back. "He'll be okay. Go." He pointed toward the bedroom.

She ran along the hallway. Dick sprawled on the floor with a silver letter opener in his chest. She couldn't imagine how Delphine could have gotten the drop on a vampire.

Amy was still oblivious in the bed and Betsy—who was obviously Delphine—stood on the other side of the bed with an open pair of scissors to her own throat.

The possessed woman snarled. "Let me go or I'll take your precious Betsy with me."

"What would be the point of that?" She shook her head and took a step forward.

"To break his heart." Her smile was malicious as she glanced at the vampire.

She could only imagine how strong and fast the woman was now—strong enough and fast enough to take down a vampire. She touched the scar and said, "Sleep."

Delphine remained standing and stared at her with a small smirk. "She's already asleep, stupid."

Shit! Where the hell is Scott?

Lexi sensed that she didn't have long to act. She could only think of one course of action and didn't like it. She took another step toward Delphine. "I can't let you do this." She put her hands up to show the woman she wasn't armed.

The madwoman surged into an attack. The scissors lowered from Betsy's throat and pointed at the new target. Instead of pushing her attacker back, Lexi pulled the woman toward her and they landed hard. The scissors plunged into her stomach, and Delphine grinned.

She flailed and screamed as she slapped ineffectually at the woman's arms, while her assailant yanked the scissors out and held them over her.

Lexi tried to speak.

Delphine leaned closer. "What are you trying to say, honey?"

She drew in a ragged breath. "I got you…right where I want you."

Her fingers closed around the necklace and she tugged hard. It snapped and slipped from Betsy's neck.

The scissors fell when the arthritis in her eighty-year-old fingers made them too difficult to hold.

The woman screamed in horror. "No! What is this?"

Scott appeared behind her and pulled the ring from her hand.

"You took your time," Lexi whispered.

"I was healing Broullard. I can't be everywhere at once."

"I bet you could." Dick coughed and blood sprayed over his shirt. He wiped it and avoided the letter opener that still protruded from him. "Shit."

Scott crouched and faced him but the vampire pushed him away. "See to her."

The sorcerer put one hand on Lexi. A metal marble appeared in his hand but disappeared in seconds.

Broullard entered, holding towels. He passed one to Scott and moved to Dick.

"You can pull that out." The young man pointed at the letter opener.

The cop hesitated.

Dick gasped. "You're looking a little pale there, my friend."

He smirked. "We could be twins."

The vampire grasped the opener and pulled it out himself. He slumped and Broullard pressed the towel on the wound.

Lexi closed her eyes as the pain faded in her stomach.

CHAPTER FOURTEEN

Betsy watched the young woman, who gazed at the ring. It sat under an upturned glass in the middle of the table. "Are you thinking of taking it for a spin?"

Lexi looked at her with an eyebrow raised. "Would you recommend it?"

The old woman sighed and pushed down a wave of nausea. "I don't remember a thing about it. I think I'm quite happy about that."

"I wonder if Amy will remember anything." She looked curiously at the ring once more.

Betsy thought about what Amy had done to her young beau. "I hope not. Will you take the ring to the museum?" She opened the oven, removed the cookies, and put them down beside the other piles of cookies, brownies, and cupcakes that filled almost every surface in the apartment.

"We'll get Joseph to exorcize the spirit first. That is a disaster waiting to happen—again. In the meantime, we'll see where this leads us." Lexi took the key from her vest pocket and put it on the table.

The old woman gave her a plate of cookies and patted her

cheek before she walked out of the kitchen. "I hope you get your answers, dear."

The door opened to admit Scott and Dick. The young man made a beeline for the cookies on the counter with Betsy behind him. When he reached out, she smacked his hand away. "These are for the detective."

His shoulders slumped. "Again? Won't you make any for me?"

The woman stepped closer to the counter but turned to face him. "Scott dear, I promise. Whenever I stab you, you'll get cookies too."

"Well, when will that be? Because I want a cookie." He stepped closer to a tray.

"Sooner than you think if you steal one of the detective's cookies."

Scott continued to whine. "But he's not even here."

"He needed to see his wife. And maybe get away from me. But he'll be back and when he is, he'll have these waiting for him." She looked at everything she'd made. Baking relaxed her and she dearly needed something to keep her busy.

Dick gazed at the stacks of baked goods. "Nothing says 'Sorry I stabbed you' like a double chocolate chip cookie."

The sorcerer pointed at him. "You stabbed Dick. Why don't you make him cookies and I'll have them?"

The vampire pinched the bridge of his nose. "Don't get her started again. She's chased me around offering her neck for the last two hours. It's positively indecent."

Betsy twisted the corner of her apron. "I hate that you have the memory of me attacking you with a letter opener. I don't know how you can bear to look at me."

"And you think chasing me with your neck out will traumatize me less?" He rolled his eyes.

Lexi broke a cookie in half and ate it while she looked directly at Scott and made "mmmm" sounds.

A whine filled the air and the old woman looked at the puppy. "What's wrong, Marcel?"

"That was Scott." Lexi chuckled.

Betsy looked at him as he sighed pathetically over a pile of the delicious-smelling baked goods. "Fine. One. You may have one cookie because you didn't let anyone die."

He put an arm around her. "I know it's been said before, but it wasn't your fault. I healed Broullard, Lexi, and Dick within minutes and no one blames you."

She plastered a big smile onto her face. "It's kind of you to say that, Scott. Really, everyone, I'm fine." She felt every one of her eighty years.

Dick lifted her chin. "It's good to hear it. And I hope your dance card isn't full because I plan to take you out tonight."

"You're very sweet, dear, but I think I've had as much excitement as I'll ever need. I'm ready to see my son and go home."

The vampire took her hand. "How about dinner, then?"

"Yes, dinner would be lovely. Somewhere quiet."

"I want to point out that this"—Scott held the cookie up—"is the price Betsy put on me saving your lives. One cookie… between you. Remember that."

The old woman snatched the cookie away. "And that's why you can't have nice things."

Dick picked his jacket up. "Okay, we'll see where the key leads, then I'd be delighted to escort you to dinner."

Betsy waved goodbye as they left. The door closed and she allowed the smile to fade from her face. She looked around the apartment and sighed. It had been quite an adventure, except for stabbing everyone. After she checked on the tray of cookies in the oven, she walked to the balcony and looked out. It was dark, and mosquitos were becoming a pest. She drew the screen across the doors and looked at Marcel. He'd fallen asleep on the floor no more than two steps away from his dinner. She turned her head at a knock at the door, slipped the necklace below her neckline, and opened it.

The young man smiled. "Is William here?"

"I'm afraid you've just missed him. Are you Peter?"

He nodded shyly. "Yes, ma'am."

She stepped back and opened the door a little wider. "Come in. How are you feeling now?"

"I'm…much better, thank you." He took her hand quickly and kissed it. "I didn't know William was hiding the most stunning woman in all creation here. He's full of surprises."

Betsy smiled at the pale young man, but that comment had seemed a little forward. "Well, thank you. Would you like to wait? I'm sure he'll return soon. Can I get you a drink?"

Peter scratched his little goatee beard and glanced toward the table, then narrowed his eyes at the upturned glass over the ring. His face expressed puzzlement. He dragged his gaze back to her. "That's very kind of you." His head tilted toward the glass. "Hmm!"

"Excuse me, I have to check on my cookies." She returned the oven and stooped to look through the oven door before she felt a chill as though the man stood incredibly close—directly behind her, perhaps—and her heart raced. At Marcel's growl, she straightened and began to turn. The apartment door opened and her three friends entered.

"Don't look at me. It's your key. Why didn't *you* pick it up?" Dick shook his head.

Betsy shook her head when she realized she was alone in the kitchen. "Peter?" She looked around in bewilderment. "Dick, your friend Peter is here."

The vampire smiled. "He is? Peter?" There was no answer.

She stared at the swaying screen across the balcony doors. "I don't understand. He was here. I spoke to him not three seconds before you opened that door."

Marcel continued to growl, this time near the balcony.

Lexi and Dick shared a look.

"What did he look like?" the vampire asked

Betsy shrugged. "Handsome, pale. Long dark hair and one of those tiny little beards they wear these days."

"Lorenzo," Lexi and Dick said together.

Scott stood at the table and picked the key up for the locator spell. "Betsy, where's the ring?"

They all spun to look at the glass in the middle of the table that no longer contained a possessed ring.

The young man put his hands on the back of a chair and stared at the glass. "This is bad."

Lexi looked at Dick. "I'll kill him."

CHAPTER FIFTEEN

"How is she?" Lexi glanced at the door as Dick entered.

He closed it behind him. "Lying down."

Scott snatched a cookie. "Even with a thirty-two-year-old body, this will take its toll. I've recommended she keep the necklace on until she's home."

Dick narrowed his eyes. "I thought it was only a glamor."

He sat on the arm of the couch. "Do you know the saying, you're only as old as you feel?"

The vampire nodded. "I see. Well, we need to get her out of here. She's not safe. I won't risk her again."

"I've messaged Dolores." The sorcerer broke the cookie in half.

Lexi twirled the mystery key in her hand. "Right. We can't simply sit here. Dick, do you have any idea where Lorenzo would go?"

"A few. But is it Lorenzo? Perhaps we should ask where *Delphine* would go."

She dug her fingertips into her forehead and screwed her face up. "Shit."

"We—" A thump at the door silenced Scott. He threw the

cookie into his mouth but spat it into his hand immediately. "That's horrible. It tastes like liver."

"That pile of cookies was for Marcel." She smirked.

"Marcel gets his own cookies?" He rolled his eyes.

Lexi drew her katana and went to look through the peephole. "It's Broullard." She opened the door.

The detective entered the apartment, his face rigid.

Scott's shoulders slumped. "Another one?"

Broullard shook his head. "*One?* No. Six. I came straight here. They were found about fifteen minutes ago."

The sorcerer made his way to the kitchen sink and washed his hands. "Who were the victims?"

"A group of tourists. They were in a courtyard behind a bar. The bodies are a mess." The man stopped speaking and he stared as Scott scrubbed his tongue with his fingernails, then seemed to recover. "Yes, well. Their throats were ripped out and every one of them was found with the head facing the wrong way."

Lexi decided it was time to break the news to him. "What color were they?"

He looked at her and raised an eyebrow. "What? But you have the ring. It can't be her. Anyway, it looked like a vamp attack to me."

She pushed her chair in. "It's Lorenzo. The vampire clan leader. He was here almost an hour ago and took the ring."

Broullard's jaw dropped. "Is everyone okay? Betsy?"

Dick, who stood at the window, turned to him. "She was here alone and she's shaken up but unharmed."

The detective exhaled sharply. "This is bad. But we know it's Delphine we're following, not Lorenzo. Her previous hosts seemed to mentally go to sleep. She didn't appear to have access to their minds."

"That's usually how it works, but I've never heard of a vampire being possessed before."

They turned to the door where Joseph stood. Lexi didn't jump this time as she'd half-expected him.

The vampire nodded to him. "When I told Betsy I was going to visit Lorenzo, she told me to have a nice time. I thought she was trying to be funny. As Delphine, she wouldn't have known Lorenzo had tried to have me killed."

"How would Lorenzo have learned about the possessed ring?" Broullard asked,

He put his suit jacket on. "She said he looked at it almost straight away and thought at the time that he was simply puzzled. An upturned glass covering a ring in the middle of the table must have looked like an odd sight."

Broullard nodded. "So, he was looking for it."

Dick stood in front of the mirror and straightened his tie. "No. She was clear that his face showed surprise."

Joseph leaned on his staff and nodded. "It called to him. That's probably how Cora found it inside the couch."

Lexi looked at everyone a little warily. "Has anyone else felt it call?"

"Evil calls to evil," he explained,

Lexi looked from him to Dick. "Really? You didn't feel a hankering to try it on?"

"Are you serious right now?" A slight hissing sound escaped from Dick's fingers. "Ow!" When he removed his hand from his tie, he was wearing the silver lion's head tie pin. He glanced at Joseph. "Old habits…"

Broullard looked puzzled. "If he wasn't after the ring, why was he here?"

The vampire took a handkerchief out and wiped flakes of burned skin from the pin. "I think he was probably here to kill Betsy."

Her jaw dropped. "After the warning I gave him?"

He nodded. "You told him I was off-limits. I'm sure he thinks my friends are still on the menu."

She moved to the window. "We need to get out there and start looking."

As the others readied themselves to leave, Broullard gazed around the room at all the cupcakes and cookies. "I hope they aren't for me. She's already given me three boxes full of them."

"Pfft!" Scott muttered.

"Someone tell her I forgive her. She'll give me diabetes." The detective shook his head as they moved to the door.

Scott looked at Lexi. "I've shielded the apartments. We need to let Betsy know we're going out but that she'll be safe. Dolores should be along shortly."

"I'll tell her." She went to the other apartment and immediately heard whispers. Someone was in the bedroom with their friend. Without hesitation, she ran through the apartment and burst through the bedroom door. Betsy and Dolores stared at her in surprise.

She put her hand on her chest. "God! I thought—" She blew a short burst of air out in relief. "I don't know what I thought. We're heading out after Lorenzo."

Dolores smiled. "We're good here."

"Aren't you going to Fae?" She was surprised.

"Betsy wants to be sure Dick's safe before she leaves."

Lexi nodded and headed out.

On the street, she asked, "Should we go to the mansion again?"

Joseph considered this. "There are other places she might also be drawn to. Do you know her previous home, detective? The antique store?"

Broullard nodded. "I know it. I've done the tour several times."

Dick stepped beside him. "I'll join you as you might need someone who can match Lorenzo's speed."

The cop glanced at his vehicle. "I'll leave my car here, then. It's only a couple of blocks and it'll be easier for you to pick up a trail."

The vampire stared at him. "I'm not a bloodhound."

Broullard stuttered an apology.

"I'm kidding. Jeez, tough crowd." Dick shook his head.

Lexi's gaze slid to Joseph. "What will you do?"

"I'll warn my people to stay off the streets." He turned and walked away into the night.

Lexi, Scott, Dick, and Broullard walked together as far as Royal Street, then separated and proceeded in opposite directions.

The vampire and detective walked down the quiet dark street.

They fell silent when they approached the antique store and found the glass door shattered.

After a hasty glance at each other, Broullard drew his gun and nodded his readiness. They stepped in carefully.

Strange shadows were cast through the store from the streetlights outside.

Furniture was positioned in three sections to create two paths through to the back. They each took a side and crept through. The cop seemed to be trying to hide his jitters, although he responded with tiny jerks of his head to every creak.

"Detective Broullard," Dick began in a conversational tone and made the man jump again. "I'm sorry, do you have a first name?"

"Charles."

"Lovely to meet you, Charles. Do you think there's any way you might regulate your heart rate? It's deafening me."

With a wry smile, Broullard stood and breathed with slow, measured breaths. "Can you smell anything?"

The vampire sniffed. "Beeswax, mothballs, and blood."

"I think my grandmother wore a perfume like that."

Broullard took another step and stumbled into a marble standing ashtray. He caught it quickly before it could fall, but the metal tray inside it rang loudly.

Dick looked at him and so didn't notice when a fist swung out of the shadows and caught his head. He fell, stunned.

A second later, Lorenzo's hand held the detective by the throat against an ornate cabinet. "I thought I already dealt with you." The voice was unusually effeminate.

The assailant sniffed at Broullard and his teeth descended. He bit into his neck but pulled away immediately. His breath came heavily and he drew his head back as he breathed in and lowered it forward as he breathed out.

Lorenzo vomited pints of blood over his captive in several heaves. He dropped the man, who skidded away while he spat in disgust and wiped the blood from his face. The possessed vampire retched blood over the furniture and floor.

"Problem, madame?"

The crazed gaze darted to Dick. "William. Your life is still forfeit," he said in a more masculine voice before he vanished.

Dick looked across the store. "Oh, dear God. Please, no." He stumbled across the space, still dizzy from the blow.

Broullard stood from where he had half-cowered. "I'm okay, the blood's not mine—"

"Not you, you idiot. This is a Louis XV gilt wood and Aubusson tapestry chair. That blood will never come out."

The man stared at him with his mouth open.

He huffed and shook his head. "Come on, then." When he reached the door, he turned. "On the bright side, Charles, if you die tonight, you'll wake up again tomorrow night with Lorenzo and Delphine as your parents."

Lexi and Scott entered the mansion, this time through the front door as it opened to allow a workman out. It was the middle of the night and the house was a hive of activity, mostly centered around the sewing room. They walked to the door of the room but didn't enter. The blood-soaked bolts of cloth were gone, as was the carpet. A team of white-clad people removed the wallpaper and painted the ceiling.

A man who had been scrubbing the floor looked at them with curiosity on his face before he stood.

Scott lifted his cell to his ear as though he were listening to someone. He looked at Lexi and held the cell to his chest. "How would *you* say it's coming along?"

Her gaze darted around the room. She screwed her face up like she was looking at the world's most fucked-up job. Her glance at the guy was intended to convey, "I have your balls in the palm of my hand right now, my friend. Do not fuck with me."

He quite understandably froze.

She shrugged. "It's coming along great."

The sorcerer returned to his cell. "Great."

The guy looked like he might faint with relief. Without a word, he dropped to his knees and continued to scrub.

They wandered away from ground zero.

Scott looked over his shoulder. "How is all this going on? The owner?"

Lexi considered the question for a moment. "Broullard probably contacted a clean-up crew that works for Kindred."

He dropped the cell into his pocket. "I can't see Lorenzo getting in here with all these people around."

She stopped and looked at him. "We did."

"Oh, right. Good point."

They continued to check the house room by room.

Finally, they stood at the stairs to the attic and peered into the dark. She found a light switch and the steps gleamed with red lights. "You have to be kidding me."

Scott sneered. "It's a little macabre."

They ascended cautiously and looked around. The room wasn't big, and it was clear that no one was there. They turned to the exit and stopped in surprise. Detective Broullard stood in front of them. He was a ghoulish sight, covered in blood almost from head to toe. Worse, he didn't speak and simply stood and stared at them.

Scott leaned closer and poked him hard in the chest.

"What the hell was that for?" the detective snapped.

The sorcerer exhaled sharply. "I thought you were an apparition. I see them sometimes just after they've passed, and if they've been hit by a truck or something, they kinda look like this." He waved his hand in the detective's general direction.

"Charles? Ahh…there you are. You found them. Excellent work."

"'Charles'?" Lexi looked suspiciously at them. "You two haven't been—"

"No! I'm a married man," Broullard protested.

Scott stared at the blood. "So, what happened to you? Let me guess, someone threw a magic stone." His gaze slid to his partner.

The cop looked perplexed. "What? Oh, you mean one of Joseph's stones. Only an idiot would use one of those."

Her friend smirked as his gaze slid sideways to her.

Dick patted Broullard on the shoulder. "The detective had the damnedest luck. Lorenzo knocked me for six, then went to feed on our friend here. But it appears he may have drained the people he killed earlier tonight. He'd gorged himself on blood and had a slight reaction."

"Slight. Yes, well." The detective grimaced.

Scott put his hand on his neck and healed the puncture wound.

Lexi asked, "Any idea where he or she might have gone next?"

The vampire raised an eyebrow. "That's another thing. It's not only her in there. Lorenzo is conscious and he spoke to me. Also, he is very, very strong." He rubbed the back of his head.

Scott nodded. "It makes sense when you consider what Amy was able to do to Jamal."

She sighed. "That's disappointing news. I hoped she'd wander into the sun and burst them both into flames. If Lorenzo's awake in there, he won't let her do that."

"That ring is like the gift that keeps on giving, isn't it?" Dick turned to the stairs.

Broullard looked at his watch in horror. "Dick, look at the time. You have less than fifteen minutes to get out of the sun."

Lexi rolled her eyes. *Dick keeps forgetting the time. He'll blow his cover.*

The vampire headed down the stairs. "Yes, gosh. I absolutely must run. The furniture in this place is giving me a migraine anyway." In an instant, he was gone.

The detective looked at her. "Do vamps get migraines?"

She shrugged "Hell if I know. Shall we make a move?"

Broullard bit his lip. "Hey, I have an idea. It's fifteen minutes until sunrise—"

"Twelve," Scott interjected.

"Why don't we simply wait twelve minutes." The man sounded exhausted.

Lexi knew exactly how he felt. "Okay. Let's do a last check around the house on the way down."

As they descended the stairs, they bumped into the man who had been working on the floor. He stepped away at the sight of Broullard, who flashed his badge. The man hurried around them.

The detective scowled at his clothing. "I'm running out of shirts."

They returned to the apartment building and he climbed into his car.

Scott and Lexi climbed the stairs, stumbled into the apartment, and fell onto their beds. Both were asleep in seconds.

CHAPTER SIXTEEN

A thump at the door woke Lexi from an all too short sleep. By the time the caller knocked a second time, she was opening it.

Broullard didn't look like he'd had much sleep, but he spun fast enough and gaped at the sight of her in a vest and panties with a katana in her hand. "Sorry. Downstairs in ten. Five if you can."

She shuffled into the bedroom and poked Scott. "We're up."

He groaned. "What time is it?"

"It's best you don't know." She dragged her leathers on. "It'll only upset you."

The sorcerer looked at himself. "Eurgh! I'm still in my clothes." He stared at her as she pulled her boots on. "When did you get undressed?"

Startled, she stopped and wrinkled her brow in thought before she shook her head slowly. "I don't remember."

The two of them were at the front of the building in six minutes.

Lexi looked at the detective. "You look like you didn't get much sleep."

Broullard rubbed his face. "I didn't get any. Neither, it seems, did Lorenzo. While we were in the mansion, he was…busy."

They scrambled into his car and arrived at a bar two streets away only minutes later.

Several people had gathered outside, some with curious faces and others worried. A woman caught Lexi's arm.

"Please, is my daughter in there? I mean…she passed, we know that. But is there any way to tell if she was there?"

Someone else came forward and pulled the woman away. The witch was adorned in pentacles and goddess symbols and clearly felt she had to pull the woman away from the Kindred bitch for her safety.

Scott looked at all the worried faces. "Who are all these people?"

Broullard marched forward. "Word gets around. It's not even an official crime scene yet."

"I can see that." There was no crime scene tape and the people guarding the door looked like the clean-up crew from the mansion.

They entered the back room. The desiccated remains of at least thirty vampires lay in fragile piles around the room.

"It looks like there was a hell of a battle," Scott muttered.

The detective looked at him and shook his head. "This is all one clan."

"You're sure?" Lexi made her way around piles of ash. Some were still vaguely in the shape of a person.

Broullard nodded. "It was a massacre."

"Were there any witnesses?" She approached a table with wallets and purses piled on top and sifted through them.

"A few people from the bar out front said one man went in and came out again about twenty minutes later."

"Lorenzo? Alone? Are you sure?" Scott appeared to be struggling to believe it.

She dropped a wallet onto the pile. "How do you know which wallet came from which pile?"

Broullard shrugged. "I don't."

His answer annoyed her but she decided to leave it for now. She turned to Scott. "Find out what her name was."

She was talking about the daughter of the woman outside. He nodded once and left the room.

"I guess the war's over," the other man muttered.

Lexi turned to him. "What?"

"They've been at it for years, haven't they? I guess that's been resolved. No one will stand against his clan now."

She walked to a couple of sheets that covered human bodies. He glanced at them. "Donors."

At a loss for words, she stood, turned slowly, and took it all in. Her gaze stopped at red, floor-length drapes. "What's behind the drapes?"

Broullard glanced at them. "That's the stage area when they have live bands." He pointed in the opposite direction with his thumb. "The guys are waiting to get started."

"The guys?" She turned to see the people in white overalls. They had a large industrial vacuum and uncoiled the cables and plugged them in. She knew what this meant.

Scott was on his way in. He had also stopped to stare at them, his face horrified. He continued to walk toward Broullard and Lexi but she marched toward the men and strode straight past her friend.

She stopped in front of the white-clad men. "Unplug that and get it out of here. I want you here with a dustpan and brush. Take pictures, then bag and tag each pile separately. Where possible, I want to see each bag with some form of ID." She turned away.

One of the men called after her. "Wait. You want us to bag them separately? Why?"

Lexi halted and allowed her expression to settle into cold and inscrutable. Her companions' body language indicated that they saw the difference. She had called on her inner Kindred bitch. As she spun to the man, she heard Broullard speak to Scott. "She won't kill him here in front of everyone, will she?"

Ignoring him, she faced the man and opened her mouth to speak.

He almost stumbled over his words. "I'll do that now. Right now."

The men scrambled to remove their equipment.

Broullard exhaled a tension-filled breath. "I'm sorry. If there are new procedures we weren't aware of—"

"There are people outside—family members. We won't give them the contents of a vacuum cleaner and ask them to take a scoopful. Where possible, we will give them the remains of their loved ones. Scott."

He jumped. "Sorry, yes?"

"I want each of those wallets and purses with the correct remains. And let that woman know if her daughter is here."

Lexi turned to the detective. "Was the clan leader here?"

Broullard shook his head. "Thomas? He wasn't identified as being among the remains."

"Are you sure? There are remains unaccounted for with no ID."

"The clothes aren't a fit." The man seemed confident.

Lexi pinched her bottom lip as she thought. "Maybe Lorenzo intentionally chose a time when Thomas wasn't here to teach him a lesson?"

He scowled but thought about it. "I doubt it. You know what he's like—he'd rather simply kill people. Although he was never really a fan of getting his own hands dirty."

"You've seen that he's being influenced by Delphine now. I think he'll be fairly hands-on from here on."

Scott moved between the various piles of dust with the personal effects and muttered his locator spells. An hour later, they had almost all the names but a few vamps hadn't carried ID.

He approached Lexi with a large clear bag filled with ashes and another clear evidence bag with clothes and a small sequined coin purse.

"Thanks. Can you take it—" She paused, looked at him, and felt him through their link. He was emotionally ragged. "I'll do it." She took the bags, went outside, and squinted in the daylight to look across the sea of faces. Her gaze finally settled on the woman, whose face crumpled when she realized instantly what this meant.

She walked to her and gave her the bags. The mother held them in her arms and leaned against a man as she sobbed. Lexi glanced up and saw the witch staring at her as she returned to the bar.

When she returned, the tagging work was almost complete. She glanced around the room to ensure nothing had been missed and narrowed her eyes at the long stage drapes.

Those drapes moved. I'm sure of it.

Lexi turned to the cleaners. "Wait outside but don't go anywhere."

As they filed out, she glanced at Broullard and Scott, who both watched her curiously.

When the door closed, she pointed to the top of the drapes. Something moved very slightly on the far side.

The detective narrowed his eyes. "That area was searched."

She drew her katana and Broullard his gun. They walked hesitantly forward.

"Wait." Scott muttered a few words and the drapes separated.

Something moved among the stage lights but was difficult to make out. Lexi focused and tilted her head in concentration.

A tangle of people tied up?

They walked forward and Scott untied a rope to lower it slowly.

Broullard stared. "I think I might throw up."

What faced them was horrific. A vampire's arms, legs, back, and head had been broken and twisted to unusual angles. Long, silver-plated pins had been driven through the joints to ensure that when they set at the unusually fast speed a vampire healed at, it would appear unnatural. He looked like a crab. His eyes were full of terror and his mouth had been stitched closed with silver wire.

The sorcerer put his hand on the victim's head and he lost consciousness.

"Can you do anything about this?" Lexi asked him.

"I'll sort the silver out, for now, then I might need someone strong to help me fix this mess." He retrieved a metal ball from his pocket. "I'll plate the silver in steel and pull it out."

She took the metal ball from his palm. "Why didn't you do that in Palm Springs instead of using my gold ring?"

"I didn't know if it would work. I've been reading up since then."

Lexi dropped the ball into Scott's hand. He flicked a finger out and the drapes began to close.

They left him on the stage behind the heavy curtains and she went to the door and called the cleaner in from the bar. He approached her nervously.

"There's a witch outside with purple hair. I'd like to speak to her." She watched him walk out through the front area.

"I think you're wrong about this war being over," she said and turned to Broullard. "I have a horrible feeling it's only just begun."

He sat on the edge of a table. "Is there any chance we could get more Kindred into town to head this off?"

She sighed. "About that—"

"Get your hands off me, you motherfuckers."

She turned as the man in white overalls and two of his cronies dragged the witch in with her arms behind her back.

Her eyes widened. "What the fuck are you doing?"

"You said—"

"I said I wanted to speak to her, not fucking interrogate her. Get out of here." She half-drew her katana and they ran.

Lexi didn't like the suspicious way people looked at her because they thought she was Kindred but she missed being able to terrify pricks like that. She turned to Broullard. "I'll drop those fuckers into the Mississippi."

That's a few too many fucks. I need to get a grip. She breathed slowly for a few moments.

A little calmer, she approached the woman. "Do you have anyone here?"

The witch rubbed her arms. "No family. Probably some friends."

"I can't stay here," she continued. "We have this sicko to catch. The remains are bagged and being labeled, along with personal effects. Can you help those people outside find their loved ones?"

A cold stare was the initial response. "I don't know what you think—"

"I can help." The girl's mother entered, still cradling the bags she had given her. She handed them to her husband and his shoulders slumped as he turned away. The woman moved to the first bag and the purple-haired witch joined her. She read the tags.

Broullard put a hand on Lexi's shoulder. "I'll see she has everything she needs." He went to her.

Scott came through the drapes and vaulted down from the stage. He approached Lexi and ensured they couldn't be overheard.

She looked at the drapes. "How is he?"

"He's at Dick's apartment."

"Good. Let's get a move on."

The detective returned. "I'll oversee the rest of this process and catch up with you later."

The woman seemed to have her task in hand and now had a notepad and pen and appeared to be writing a list of names.

With their work there complete, the two friends walked to the apartment.

CHAPTER SEVENTEEN

Betsy greeted them with coffee as they entered.

"You won't believe how much I need this." Lexi was halfway through the drink before she pulled it away from her mouth to breathe.

Scott finished his coffee. "Are you ready?"

She sighed and nodded.

The older woman sat and picked the puppy up. "I'll stay right here with Marcel." No one could blame her.

The sorcerer scratched the dog behind the ears. He looked at Betsy. "The apartment is still shielded. You're safe, but if you need us, Dick will be listening."

They entered the vampire's apartment. He had moved the couch to the side of the room and Thomas remained in the middle of the floor, unconscious with his broken, crab-like limbs.

Lexi shuddered. "The way his head is twisted—it's grotesque."

Dick stared at her with an eyebrow raised.

She glanced at him. "What?"

"What do you think I looked like when you broke my neck? I had to have it re-set and I didn't have a mage to keep me unconscious."

Her grimace was genuine. "Oh. I feel bad about that, but it wasn't my fault. I was hyped-up on vamp blood."

"Yes. As I recall, that was *my* vamp blood."

"Yeah, I guess." Lexi shrugged. "Sorry, Dick."

Scott put a hand on both of their shoulders. "Well, we can all laugh about it now."

They both glared at him.

He looked pointedly at Thomas. "Let's get on with this, then. I'll break the bones where they were broken by Delphenzo. You two twist them into position and hold them in place until they start mending."

"Delphenzo." She rolled her eyes.

"Yes, it's a cross between—"

"I know. Stop speaking." She took one of Thomas's arms and they began to reset the joints and bones.

While they worked, Lexi looked at Dick. "I don't understand this place. Everywhere else I've been, when someone's turned, they leave and stay dead to their families. Here, the family seems to board the windows in their old bedroom and change breakfast time. So many humans are aware of the supernatural world here."

He nodded. "It gets stranger than that. Mothers sometimes allow their vampire kids to feed off them." He shuddered. "It gives me the heebie-jeebies."

Scott frowned. "Why?"

"It's like..." The vampire seemed to try to find the right words. "You know when you hear about women who breastfeed their kids until they're seven or eight?"

"Okay. I hear you." The young man signaled that he didn't need to hear any more.

They twisted the victim's head the right way. Like every other bone and joint they'd worked on, it cracked and crunched.

Lexi looked directly at Dick. "I really am sorry."

"I forgive you." He mussed her hair with his knuckles while she held Thomas's head in place.

She narrowed her eyes. "But if you ever do that again, I'll break your neck all over again."

"And just like that, our little moment's over." He poured himself a drink.

They moved Thomas onto the couch as a knock sounded at the door.

"It's Broullard."

Dick went into his bedroom as she opened the front door.

The detective stepped in. "How's Thomas?"

"Sleeping but otherwise, possibly in good shape."

"Let's be honest. I think any shape is preferable to the one we found him in." He smiled a humorless smile.

Lexi let him in, and he looked over the couch at Thomas. "Will he walk?"

"If we did it right." Scott yawned.

"Don't. Just...please don't yawn." Broullard sighed. "So, are you busy?"

Scott shook his head. "Another one? For the love of..."

Lexi stood outside Mardi Gras World and stared at a boat that had crashed into what appeared to be a short boarding dock. The vessel had been tied off and a cordon placed around the area. Scott had walked a little farther to see the front of it.

"Anything?"

He shrugged. "The boat's called *A Stone's Throw*."

Broullard held a little notepad. "Has the ring been here?"

The sorcerer nodded.

She boarded and waited while her two companions stepped behind her. "I'm not really into nautical...anything. Is this a shrimping boat?"

"Yes, although the owner appears to have been in the business of fishing for crabs. These are crab traps." The detective pointed out several net-covered tunnels on the deck.

"Do you know who the victims are?" She poked around a few boxes on the deck.

"The captain and four tourists. We have IDs for the tourists but I'm waiting for registration details to come back on the owner. Until then, he's merely Crab Boat Guy."

Lexi shrugged. "So, where are they?"

Broullard steadied himself as the boat rocked. "The tourists are below deck and he's in the pilothouse."

"The what?"

He rolled his eyes. "The front part." He extended his hand to stop Scott from following her. "Do you mind staying here?"

The young man sat on a deck bench. "No part of me minds that. I'm sorry I threw up at your other crime scene."

She expected the detective to follow her but instead, he sat as well. "I'm not much of a boat person. If I go in there, I'll seriously disturb *this* crime scene."

Lexi rolled her eyes and made her way past winches and nets to the pilothouse. She could see why he thought it was Lorenzo. The head had been turned one hundred and eighty degrees so the body lay on its back but the head was face-down. There wasn't much to look at. Peeking her head out the door, she saw her two companions in conversation, so she decided to have a look under the body. She could always blame the rocking of the boat.

She caught Crab Boat Guy and turned him onto his front. The man's lips moved.

Shit, he's alive.

Instinctively, she drew in a breath to call Broullard to get the paramedics when a horde of tiny crabs escaped between the lips of the corpse and scuttled across the deck.

The back of her hand slapped over her mouth, she straightened hastily. After a few seconds, the compulsion to vomit had mostly left her. She flipped the body back as she'd found it and returned to take her place with Team Vomit at the other end of the boat.

"Are you okay?" Scott was concerned. He'd have felt her emotional shift.

Carefully, she sat beside Broullard before she tried to speak. "Is there any point to me looking at the tourists?"

"I guess not. They're the same as those in the courtyard—heads twisted and throats ripped out."

They disembarked by silent consensus. Once on land, Scott muttered a few words. "The ring went this way." He pointed toward Mardi Gras World. "Do you want to follow it?"

Lexi chewed her lip, then shook her head. "Honestly, I think we need backup."

Broullard nodded. "Will you come to the station?"

"Not yet. We need to do a little research and will catch up with you."

"Can I drive you?"

"No, we need to see some people."

Back at the apartment, they heard Dick and Betsy from the stairs.

"Tell me what you need and I'll get it for you."

"I merely want a few things. Come in with me if you're so concerned."

"I don't think you comprehend the danger you would be in."

The two friends hesitated outside the door before Scott spoke the shared thought. "Should we simply go—"

Dick called out to them. "Come in."

Lexi opened the door. "If this is a bad time…"

Betsy stood from the couch. "Don't be silly, dear, this is your apartment. Good heavens, you look exhausted. I'll put coffee on."

The sorcerer yawned. "I'm going to lie down."

"We need to talk." Lexi pulled him back by the collar.

"Urgh!" He dropped into a chair and put his head on the table. "I'm listening."

"Where's Dick?" Betsy looked around the room. "Has he—Oh, for goodness sake!"

The younger woman looked toward the apartment door. "If you don't mind me asking, what's going on?"

Betsy rolled her eyes. "Dick won't let me go into our apartment. He seems to think Thomas might tear my head off or something." She scooped coffee into the machine.

Scott lifted his head. "He might. He lost considerable blood. He'll want to replace that, possibly with yours."

"Oh! I thought he was being over-protective." She blushed.

Dick walked in with her belongings. "I'm being the right amount of protective. There you go—everything you could possibly need." He looked at Lexi. "What's your problem?"

She sighed. "We need backup. Kindred backup. I'll have to tell Broullard we're not Kindred."

He grimaced. "Oh dear. That'll be an awkward conversation. Can I come?"

Her death stare, unfortunately, did nothing to diminish his humor.

CHAPTER EIGHTEEN

The two friends walked along Royal Street toward the police station.

Scott stepped behind Lexi to allow a couple to pass, then moved beside her again. "What will you say to Broullard?"

"I'll simply tell him we don't have the backing of Kindred and there is no Kindred cavalry riding toward New Orleans on shiny freaking horses."

"Can't we...uh, leave him a note? I can't see this going down very— Hey!"

She grabbed him and shoved him through the closest door and into an art gallery. Once safely inside, she yanked him against the wall between the door and the window. "Am I seeing things? I'm seeing things, aren't I?"

He peeked out and darted his head behind cover again. It must have taken a moment for him to process what he'd seen because he immediately looked out again. His jaw dropped.

Lexi took a breath and looked again. It was undoubtedly Caleb. "Who did we kill in Cabo?"

"Can I help you?" The assistant looked ready to throw the two of them out of the gallery.

"We're looking for a gift but the guy it's for is right across the street."

"Oh my, that's awkward." The man looked out. "Is it for the chief of police?"

"Yes." Scott led the man into the store.

She ignored them and peered out again. Utterly confused, she dragged her gaze from the miraculously not dead sorcerer to the man who stood with him. Even more startled, she retrieved the photograph of herself in Jackson Square.

Her friend moved beside her and she glanced at the assistant, who stood with a smile on his face and an unfocused look in his eyes and stared in the direction of a wall. She showed Scott the photo. "It's him. It's the guy from the picture."

He looked out again. The man across the street with Caleb was in uniform. "He's the chief of police? He must be Kindred. If he is, why would he talk to an evil sorcerer?"

"Caleb manipulated the whole of Palm Springs. It's not a stretch to guess he's done it here too."

She glowered through the window and grasped the hilt of the katana in her pocket. "I want to know what they are saying."

"Okay." The sorcerer muttered a few words and in a moment, they were able to hear the conversation.

"And I have a problem with my pet vampire," the chief blustered. "Lorenzo has way overstepped the mark. The agreement was that we'd let him gain a block. He was supposed to help us cull the shifters, then go after Carla's clan. There's only six of them but they style themselves after a family. Somehow, he eliminated Thomas and his entire clan, including a couple of human donors. He wasn't sanctioned for that."

"How's your girl doing with the other investigation?" Caleb's voice made her shudder.

"I spoke to her yesterday. She's wrapping things up. There was definitely magic at play. The security camera's suddenly on the fritz and no one remembers seeing it."

"It doesn't matter. I know who the culprits are, or at least know one of them." He laughed. "I still can't quite believe it. She's not quite the harmless old bird I thought she was."

"I'll rip her eyeballs out," a guttural voice exclaimed.

Visions of Betsy being tortured and screaming assaulted Lexi's mind. She held her head as the images became more obscene until suddenly, they were gone. Shaken, she stared at Scott, who had clearly seen the same and protected them from it. He leaned heavily against the wall with his eyes closed before he returned her gaze. She peeked out of the gallery window to where Caleb pinched the bridge of his nose.

She opened her mouth to speak but he shook his head quickly. Instead, she mouthed, "Azatoth?"

Scott nodded.

The conversation outside the station continued.

"Are you all right, Caleb?" The chief sounded concerned.

"I'm fine—it's a headache."

"Please, my lord, I can't think." The man's voice sounded weary.

"I am closer. Soon, I will be with you."

Caleb's voice was strained when he tried to continue his conversation. "I've been busy but I'll locate her tonight and send friends over. How is it going with the shifters?"

"Lorenzo hasn't moved on them yet. He's doing it tomorrow night."

"Good. We'll chastise him after he's taken care of the shifters and the witches. The supernatural population in New Orleans has grown out of all proportion. We need this cull."

The two friends looked at each other. She was keen to get out of there.

The chief continued, "That reminds me—Broullard has dealt with things while I've been away. I passed him in the hallway a few minutes ago. I haven't had a sit-down with him yet, but he's asking awkward questions. Should I arrange to have him counseled again?"

The Kindred term raised Lexi's eyebrow. The official was definitely Kindred, then. But why did he take orders from Caleb? Was he yet another person under the sorcerer's thrall?

"No. Find a reason to send him to the bayou with the shifters. He'll be collateral damage. Keep me informed."

He climbed into a waiting car and drove away. The chief remained outside.

Scott exhaled sharply. "That was intense."

She wiped her brow. "Those visions. How did we see them?"

"We picked up all communication from where they were standing. I didn't specify the frequency." He shuddered. "So, he still has that demon in his head. And I bet it's really pissed after not crossing over."

Lexi rubbed at the goosebumps on her arms. "What do you think he meant by 'soon, I will be with you.' I thought he wouldn't get near our dimension for hundreds of years."

"I don't know. But it's very clear what Caleb's plan for Betsy is. We should get back to the apartment. I need to protect her."

They left the gallery as the man on the steps looked up. He raised his eyebrows in surprise and stared directly at her for a moment before he raised his arm to make a come-here signal with two fingers. She looked around in the hope that he had targeted someone else.

Scott prodded her back. "We have to go over there. If it gets difficult, I'll send him to sleep."

She approached the man and opened her mouth to deliver a vague greeting.

He spoke first. "I thought you were in Cabo."

"I...I was." She wondered how he knew she had been there.

"I wasn't expecting you here yet. When did you get back?"

"Just now." She was winging it.

Who does this guy think I am?

He stretched an arm out, took hold of a railing, and looked around. She realized he was waiting for a couple to walk past.

His voice lowered. "Do you have any leads on who killed the doppelgänger?"

"Nope." She saw his eyes narrow at her brief response. "I'm waiting for results from the lab."

"Make sure your paperwork's in order. When the head of the Kindred council asks specifically for you, it could mean big things for your career. You just missed him, by the way. And I'm fine, thanks for asking."

"I was about to," she told him and shrugged.

The chief continued. "Palm Springs was a shit-fest. There were hundreds of the buggers. One of them broke my glasses and I can't see for shit. I barely recognized you from across the street."

He held a hand up with a bandaged finger. It looked shorter than it should have been. She noticed one of his other fingers was also missing a tip, an older injury. "He's talking about wanting another one. Son of a bitch. The perks of the job aren't worth this."

Lexi nodded as though she had a clue about what was going on.

"Who's that?" He pointed to Scott, who remained a discreet distance away and looked around with a vaguely disinterested expression.

Despite the natural instinct to do so, she didn't look at him. "He's…going to look at my car."

"I see. You're getting straight back into things then. I only recently got back myself and it looks like shit's been going down here. You can't leave them alone for five minutes." He raised a hand and she froze while he tucked a lock of her hair behind her ear. "You look nice. Cabo must have agreed with you. I thought you weren't going to hide your scars again."

It came so suddenly that she freaked out on the inside, her mind a whirlwind. "You know what they say about Cabo."

"I better not get a bar bill. Anyway, I have stuff to do." The man headed up the steps, then turned to her again. "Stay in the apartment. It's best you're not seen on the street yet."

"Yes, sir." She waited until she was sure he had entered the station.

Lexi turned to Scott. "Let's get the hell out of here."

His face was perplexed. "Who did he think you were?"

"Message Dolores. We need to see her."

At the apartment, Dick and Betsy were waiting when they entered.

The vampire stood. "How did Charles take the news?"

Lexi marched around the room. "I need a drink. Is Dolores here yet?"

"I didn't know we were expecting her."

The older woman slid off the stool at the breakfast bar. "I'll put a pot of—"

"No thanks. Dick?"

"Coming right up." Although he looked surprised, he disappeared and returned with a bottle of Jack Daniels. He poured a large drink for her and she threw it back. She stood and breathed slowly with her eyes closed for a few moments as she tried to slow her racing heart. Wordlessly, she held the glass out to him. He raised an eyebrow but refilled it.

As she lifted the glass, she thought better of it. With a sigh, she put it down. "I need to contact Joseph. Should I simply say his name three times into the mirror?"

Dick wiggled his cell phone at her. "Or I could call him for you."

"That sounds reasonable." She turned to Scott. "What message did you send to Dolores?"

"I told her we need to speak to her."

"Send her a nine-one-one."

He took his cell again out.

Lexi turned to Betsy. "I'm sorry, but you need to get your stuff together."

The vampire gazed intently at her. "What's going on?"

"Do you know what a doppelgänger is?" she asked him.

Dick's brow furrowed. "Theoretically."

"That's what we killed in Cabo." She focused on Betsy. "Caleb's still alive and he's coming after you. He'll try to locate you but the attack could be physical or psychic. I think it's best to move you to Fae." She grinned when Betsy downed the shot on the counter.

Dick was a blur. In seconds, he had already moved two of the woman's cases into the room while messaging Joseph.

Lexi thought for a moment, then spoke to him. "There are a few other people I need here. I imagine Joseph could help us with that if he feels like it. How's Thomas?"

"It's about time for him to wake up. It might help to contain the situation if the first thing he sees is a Kindred legacy holding something long and pointy."

"Bring Betsy. I don't want her out of my sight, but I want both of you to stand between her and Thomas when he wakes up." She led the way to the other apartment and they waited for the vampire to open his eyes. After a few moments, they were joined by Dick and Betsy, who held the glass and bottle.

She expected the healed vampire to spring into action, but when his eyes opened, he merely lay there and stared at the ceiling.

Her first thought was that he might be paralyzed. "Can you move?"

He nodded slowly. "Are they all gone?"

"Everyone who was there," Scott answered. "All the vampires and a couple of donors."

Dick stood with Betsy behind him. "I have some blood bags. Is that okay for you?"

"I'm good, thanks." Thomas continued his fixed stare.

Lexi wondered if she'd misunderstood his response. "You lost considerable—"

"I lost everything. You should have let me go."

She decided she didn't have time for this. "You can meet the sun when Lorenzo's dead."

He barked a laugh, then looked at her. "I don't think you know what you're dealing with."

"We know exactly what we're dealing with, and we need all the help we can get. Dick, get the blood."

In Lexi's apartment, the fae door appeared. She leapt to her feet and walked to it. Her boss entered the room and the portal behind her vanished.

"What do you know about doppelgängers?" the girl asked immediately.

Dolores straightened her already pristine skirt suit and placed her purse on the table. "I know they're difficult to make. It takes thirteen sorcerers."

Scott looked at Lexi. "Thirteen mages. The Kindred council."

"Well, Kindred outlawed the practice but that's probably why there were originally thirteen on the council. There are several spells, all of which require thirteen." The woman looked at him. "You don't know any of this?"

He blushed. "I guess I missed that day at Mage School."

She sighed. "It's advanced and the details of the spell-work, like everything else in that ridiculous organization, is quite secretive. But I do know this—the magic requires that the sorcerers participating in a spell to create a doppelgänger each have to donate a piece of themselves. Traditionally, the tip of a finger."

Lexi nodded. "We've seen the chief of police. He's Kindred

and two of his fingers were missing their tips. One recent and bandaged, and the other had long healed."

Scott shook his head. "The chief wasn't a sorcerer. I'd have known."

"Each sorcerer can use a proxy," the fae explained. "Whom do you suspect of being a doppelgänger?"

The girl sat heavily. "Caleb's not dead, he's after Betsy, and it looks like he might be the head of the Kindred council."

"At least, that's what the chief thinks," Scott added. "We know how manipulative Caleb can be."

Dolores's eyebrows raised in alarm. "The head of the Kindred council tried to release a high-level demon from a hell dimension?"

"*Is* trying. It's still in his head. We eavesdropped and heard it telling him it was getting closer." Lexi stood. "What does that mean? I thought the portal to that dimension couldn't open here for hundreds or thousands of years."

The woman thought for a moment. "He might try to make his way through other dimensions. How did Betsy take it?"

"She's through here." She led her boss to the other apartment where Dick was seated on the couch and Thomas in the chair opposite.

"Good evening, William." Dolores smiled. As she approached the couch, she noticed Betsy asleep on his shoulder, cradling the half-empty bottle of Jack Daniels.

"I see." She sighed, retrieved her cell, and typed a short message.

Lexi shook her head. "I don't understand. Okay, he looked exactly like Caleb—which is kind of the point, I suppose. But he sat up before I took the shot and looked directly at Betsy, and I would swear he recognized her. Azatoth has some revolting plans for her, by the way."

Betsy straightened suddenly. "Caleb *and* Azatoth can kiss my wrinkly old butt." She slumped against Dick's arm again. He tried to use the opportunity to maneuver the bottle out of her hold but she wouldn't release it.

Dolores pocketed her cell. "A sorcerer can maintain a psychic link with the doppelgänger. He probably watched out of the creature's eyes."

The inebriated woman began to snore and Dick slid the bottle gently out of her hand. "What exactly is a doppelgänger?" he asked softly. "I mean, what is it made from?"

"It's a human, usually chosen for their size and shape." The fae took the bottle from his hand and put it on a table. "Sometimes, but not always, they are a willing participant. The mind is wiped and replaced and the face altered by the spell."

Lexi shook her head as she mentally replayed the shot she'd taken at Caleb's heart. "Is the original always mentally linked to the copy and aware?"

"No, that would only happen if the original was a sorcerer. When the transformation is complete, the doppelgänger believes they are the original."

She drew in a deep breath. "We have another problem. I think there's another doppelgänger out there and I think it's a copy of me. Since we got here, every supernatural creature in town has known who I am. I thought it was because a group of shifters had seen my scar."

Scott's jaw dropped. "Detective Broullard. At the crime scene, you said he didn't ask your name or ask for ID. But there can't be one of me because no one seems to know who I am."

"And when I picked this vest up from Anne Bird's store…" Lexi turned to Dolores. "You didn't send this to Anne Bird for me." It wasn't a question, but the woman shook her head anyway.

"So that key we found in the pocket—" the sorcerer started.

"Must belong to the doppelgänger," she finished.

She yanked the photo from her pocket and held it up. "This isn't me."

Her boss took the photograph and studied it. "Did you find out who the man is?"

"That's the chief of police. He's older now, of course, but easily recognizable."

"The man missing the tips of his fingers." The woman exhaled, her expression grim.

Lexi nodded. "He thinks I'm the doppelgänger, who Caleb specifically requested to investigate a shooting in Cabo."

Dick twisted on the couch to face them. "But why would anyone make a doppelgänger of you? Okay, no offense, but what's the point? You've said it yourself—as far as legacies go, you're a dud."

She stared at him.

He stroked an eyebrow. "Don't give me the murder face. They were your words, not mine." He propped the still snoring woman against the backrest and stood. "I'll check the other apartment for anything belonging to Betsy."

When he opened the apartment door, he stood face to chest with a huge man. He stumbled back. "Jesus!"

"Ah! Simon, there you are. Come on in." Dolores beckoned to the man who had to stoop beneath the doorframe to enter. "This is Simon. He'll help me with Betsy."

The vampire narrowed his eyes. "I can carry her."

"Dick—" The fae raised an eyebrow.

He rolled his eyes, "Et tu, Dolores."

She smiled kindly. "I'm sure you understand that the fae don't want a vampire loose over there."

"Actually, I don't. I'm fairly sure from what I've heard I'd be the least scary thing over there. Besides, you sylphs taste of ozone. Urgh!" He shuddered.

The woman leveled her gaze at him. "I won't ask how you know that."

"Dolores! I've dated fae."

"He's dated everything," Scott muttered.

The vampire fixed him with an indignant look.

Lexi remembered that Betsy's son was still in Fae. "How's Todd?"

"Todd's awake and doing very well. The fae girls are fighting over him. It's for the best that Betsy's coming over. If he stays there unchaperoned much longer, he'll come back married."

Dick smiled widely. "But fae babies are delightful. Who wouldn't want those genes in their family? It didn't do Grace Kelly any harm."

"Or Halle Berry," said a deep rich voice.

Lexi spun. "Joseph. I'd like a word with you in a moment."

Dolores created a fae door and Scott pushed the bags through. Simon walked around the couch and lifted the sleeping Betsy gently into his arms. Dick stepped forward and kissed the young-looking woman on the head, then watched as the man stepped through the portal. On the other side, he turned and held a small, frail woman in her eighties.

The vampire smiled. "It's been wonderful seeing her young again. She's the last connection to who I was."

"She'll be safe." Dolores patted his arm, then stepped through and the doorway was gone.

Lexi turned immediately to Joseph and pointed a finger at him. "You knew!"

"I did?" The man knew he wasn't fooling anyone with his innocent face.

"About the doppelgänger here—with my face. You must have known. Why didn't you say anything?"

"It's not for the rest of us to interfere in the business of Kindred. Men have been killed for less. And how do you know that *you* are not the doppelgänger?"

That comment disturbed her more than she was willing to admit.

CHAPTER NINETEEN

Aknock at the door delayed Lexi's response as she went to see who it was. She peered through the peephole at Agatha with her parents.

She opened the door and smiled. "Hello, Agatha."

The girl ran in, sat on the floor, and began to play with Marcel.

Her father sniffed. "I smell vamp—" He stopped when he saw the others around the room. After a wary moment of scrutiny, he nodded to Joseph and the couple sat at the table.

Lexi closed the door, looked at those gathered, and was a little surprised by the turnout. Scott, Dick, Joseph, Thomas were unsurprising, of course, but Anne was there with Sam and James as well. Geraldine had arrived soon after Broullard and now Agatha's parents, who were called George and Olivia. Everyone had fallen silent and stared at her, obviously waiting for her to speak. She took a deep breath.

"My name is Lexi. Well, it's Alexa but I go by Lexi. I used to be a Kindred legacy based in Texas, but I found myself at odds with their ethos and I left. This is Scott. He's my blood match." She paused to see the reactions. "Joseph already knows but the rest of you don't seem surprised."

Broullard raised his hand. "I'm surprised."

Sam stared intently at her face. "How can you look so much like Ali? Okay, you don't have the scars, but I assumed you used magic to hide them. Are you sisters?"

So that's what they call her. I wonder why they didn't steal my name along with my face.

"Scars?" she asked.

"Ali was mauled by a shifter about five years ago," Broullard explained.

Olivia nodded. "I knew she was too nice. I said as much, didn't I, George? And she smells different."

James leaned back and folded his arms. "I thought maybe Alice had a stroke. Sometimes, that can make people behave differently and even smell different than supernaturals."

"I thought she was a pod person," George added.

The scrutiny made Lexi uncomfortable and she pushed on. "Since you've mentioned pod people, you should know why I'm here. I've tried to find information about my past. I was given this photograph." She dropped it onto the table. "And I came to find out why I was here back then and who the man is."

Broullard tapped the picture. "That's my boss, the police chief."

"I know that now. I've just learned it's not me in the picture. It's a doppelgänger."

"You're Dolores' friend. I wondered why no one turned up for the documents." Anne pointed at the linen vest. "So that's not your vest."

Lexi put a hand on the garment. "No. I guess not. But I really, really like it."

James Bird shook his head. "How do we know Alice is the doppelgänger and not you? She's been here for years."

Joseph, who had leaned on the back of her chair, stood. "I can tell you with absolute certainty that Lexi is not a doppelgänger."

She twisted in the chair to look into his face. "That's not what you said earlier."

"I was only having some fun." He laughed and she bristled, feeling his joviality was inappropriate.

Everyone nodded and appeared to accept what she had said. She had imagined it would be a hard sell, but Joseph's word seemed to carry considerable weight.

"I need to tell you what I learned today. Why you're here." She leaned forward. "It seems your local Kindred unit had an arrangement with Lorenzo. They allowed him to make a play for an extra city block while they were out of town."

Broullard narrowed his eyes. "How could they know they'd be called away? Were they lying about the disaster in Palm Springs? Was it faked?"

Lexi shook her head. "No, it was orchestrated by a man we know as Caleb."

The detective's jaw dropped. "Caleb? The chief's friend? He said that Caleb guy is high up in Kindred. I'm sorry, but this sounds less plausible."

Thomas steepled his fingers and tapped them against his chin. "Lorenzo took far more than a city block."

Joseph leaned lazily against the wall. "Lorenzo is now possessed by the spirit of Delphine LaLaurie."

"Oh, shit." Sam Bird and Geraldine said at the same time.

"What he did to me kind of makes sense now." Thomas sounded hollow.

James straightened. "What did he do to you?"

The vampire refused to meet his gaze. "I don't want to talk about it."

Dick pulled his cell out, scrolled, and showed it to the man.

He stared bug-eyed at the phone. "Fuuuuuck!"

Thomas glared at his fellow vampire. "You took pictures?"

"It's evidence. I'm a PI."

Everyone looked at him.

"Well, I am." He smoothed an eyebrow.

Broullard frowned. "Licensed?"

"You say potato." Dick poured himself a glass of bourbon.

Anne Bird shrugged. "What does all this have to do with us?"

"They have something else planned. This time, it's something involving the shifters tomorrow night. They mentioned the bayou, but I don't know what they're planning." Lexi looked at Geraldine to see if it meant anything to her, but her gaze was drawn to Olivia who had covered her mouth with her hand.

"Tonight's the eve of the full moon," George answered. "The new shifters are out in the Bayou for their rite of passage. Their first change is at full moon tomorrow night. Some of them are already there. We were leaving to take Agatha when Joseph called."

Lexi was horrified. "They're already there?"

She patted Scott's arm. "Get Dolores here." She turned to Anne. "They have something planned for the witches too, but we don't know what or when."

"Why are they doing this?" James asked.

Her face screwed up in disgust. "Population control. It's a cull. Caleb has decided the supernatural community in New Orleans is too big to control."

Broullard frowned. "I don't know what you think I can do about this. If what you're saying is true, we won't be able to rely on any support from the department."

"You're here because we overheard a conversation between the chief and Caleb today. Apparently, you've asked questions— too many."

The detective raised his eyebrows. "I did bombard the chief with questions today. What am I supposed to do about that?"

Dick put a glass of bourbon in front of the man. "Pal, if I were you, I'd take a few sick days on the other side of the world."

Anne leaned forward. "How can we help?"

"Lorenzo and Delphine are the immediate problems. We need to get the possessed ring away from him. He'll be easier to deal with and taking him out of play will set Caleb's plans back. But I think it'll take more than the handful of people we have here."

Thomas rubbed his face, his expression grim. "I'll speak to the other clans. The situation has been hostile lately and I've mediated relations between them. I think I have the respect of the other leaders, but I don't have my clan behind me to watch my back anymore. It would help to have backup with me."

"Dick and I will come with you." Lexi turned to Scott. "I'll need you to help get the kids out of the bayou and keep them somewhere safe."

"It'll be difficult to protect that many people. I already have a permanent shield on us so Kindred can't find us." He checked his cell. "Dolores will be with us in a few minutes."

Sam looked at her mother. "We should touch base with the local covens. If something's coming, we need to protect ourselves or get out."

Her mother raised an eyebrow. "I won't go anywhere. They won't drive me out of town."

Joseph pushed away from the wall he'd leaned against. "I'll help with the children."

"What can I do?" Broullard stood.

Lexi exhaled sharply and shrugged. "Honestly? Take your wife and get the hell out of town."

He folded his arms. "I won't run away. This is my city too."

Scott thought about it. "I can shield you, but Caleb might be able to break through that. Now that I think about it, it's a wonder he hasn't broken through already. He's ahead of me in ability and he has demonic powers too."

"Demonic?" Sam asked.

Dick held a finger up. "Oh, right, we didn't share that part.

Caleb's working in collusion with a high-level demon called Azatoth."

"The deceiver?" Joseph shook his head. "This is very bad."

James raised an eyebrow. "He's a demon. Aren't they all deceivers?"

Lexi shared a glance with Scott. "What do you know about him, Joseph?"

"My spirits have spoken of him. He's tried to escape from the realms of hell for eons, moving through the hell dimensions. It takes years of effort on his part. He sends his mental tendrils out, trying to ensnare a creature in another realm. Once he has them, he uses them to help build his power.

"He connected briefly with a human a hundred years ago. The man had no magic and could not call the demon forth, but he was a writer. He attempted to make him use the name Azatoth in his work because names have power. His plan was to spread the name through the human world. It almost worked, but the writer had misheard the demon's name as Azathoth. To this day, that name is used the world over."

"Of course! *Call of Cthulhu*, the role-playing game?" Scott looked surprised by the revelation. "I knew it was familiar."

"Yes." The other man nodded. "And the writer was HP Lovecraft."

Dick steepled his fingers on his chin. "But now he has a sorcerer. It was our dumb luck that he didn't manage to come through last time in Palm Springs. I doubt we'll be that lucky again."

Scott looked at Lexi. "I don't think there's anything we can do about the demon right now. If Caleb tries to locate Broullard and he's not where he's supposed to be, they might be suspicious."

"Then let's make sure he's exactly where he should be." Joseph held a voodoo doll in his hand. "May I trouble you, my friend?" he asked the detective.

Broullard sighed, pulled a few strands of hair from his head, and passed them to him.

The man tucked the hairs into the doll's fabric vest. "I'll leave this in the bayou when we round the children up."

The other man swallowed. "Leave it somewhere safe."

Scott muttered a few words and announced that Broullard was shielded.

Lexi looked at Dick, whose eyes were sad as he watched Agatha play with Marcel. He glanced at Joseph in unspoken communication.

"Agatha. Can you do a very important job for me?" Joseph asked.

The girl looked up and nodded.

The old man crouched and scratched Marcel behind the ear. "Can you and your mom look after Marcel for a little while?"

She smiled. "Sure, until you kill the ghost lady."

Lexi shook her head. *Kids.*

By the time Lexi, Dick, and Thomas stepped onto the street, it was 2:00 am. The witches had already left, and the shifters had begun to ferry the children from the bayou.

They walked toward the vamp bar on Frenchman's Street.

Lexi slid her gaze to Thomas. There was nothing of the predator about him. He walked purposefully but without any real attention. She needed to bring him out of it. "Are you sure the other clans will help?"

He sighed. "Vampires are selfish by nature. Our decisions can be arbitrary. They might help, they might not."

She stepped around trash bags on the sidewalk. "Why would they hold you in particular regard? Why aren't you selfish?"

"They show me a semblance of respect because I was a priest.

Honestly, I think it simply amuses them. All except Lorenzo. He's never liked me, clearly."

Her eyes widened as she glanced at Dick before she returned her focus to Thomas. "How does that work? An ex-priest leading a vampire clan?"

"Vampires can have a crisis of faith too. I didn't really have a clan. It was more like a congregation and I didn't sire vampires. My group was made up of people who struggled with what they were. Anyway, the clan we'll see here is the second largest after Lorenzo's. Their leader, Anna, stopped all communication with the others a year ago. I'm the only vampire not of her clan that she'll speak to. She won't even hear you out without me there."

Dick clapped him on the shoulder. "Well, it's a good job we have you with us."

The other man seemed disinclined to speak after that. He walked faster to move ahead of his companions as they made their way through the streets.

As Thomas stepped out to cross the road, a sudden surge of power stole her breath. A hooded man appeared beside her with his arms outstretched. She and Dick were bathed in a blue-white light. Lexi couldn't see the man's face and before she could react, Thomas' head was detached from his body, which fell. A bright flash illuminated the street and a moment later, a boom filled the air. It could only be the sound of something fast colliding with something impenetrable. In the next moment, Lorenzo stood in front of them. He picked himself off the ground, smiled and gave her a little salute, and was gone.

Lexi turned to the hooded figure, but he was gone too.

The two companions stared at Thomas' desiccating body.

Dick caught her arm. "We need to get to the apartment."

She created a shield around them which faded and died after a few seconds. "Shit." She didn't need to look at the scar to know that it was empty.

He lifted her unceremoniously and moved at vamp speed, only stopping when they reached the door to the building.

She wriggled out of his grasp. "Let go of me."

The vampire dropped her. "I could have simply left you."

Her face flamed with shame. "It would have been preferable. Open," she commanded and held her hand out to the door. It blew into the hallway.

Dick frowned at her. "How did that work and the shield didn't?"

"I'm closer to Scott so the magic's coming back." She stormed through the entrance.

As they made their way up the stairs, she glanced at the scar which slowly filled with light. *Better late than never.*

The vampire gestured over his shoulder at the damaged door. "Aren't you going to fix that?"

Lexi stopped and gave him *the* stare.

He rolled his eyes. "Okay. I'm sorry I threw you over my shoulder like a rag doll. I panicked. I didn't even see him move and it freaked me out."

She marched down the stairs, lifted the door, and leaned it against the frame. "There, fixed."

As they entered the apartment, Broullard jumped up. "You were qui..." His voice died in his throat and he stared at their faces.

Lexi went directly to the bourbon, stared at the bottle, then sighed. She glanced speculatively at Dick.

"Hey, I'm off the menu, remember? God, you're worse than... me." He dropped into a chair and looked at the detective. "Lorenzo attacked us. He killed Thomas."

Broullard narrowed his eyes. "How in hell did you two survive?" He looked from one to the other. She ignored him and stared at the bourbon again.

The vampire answered. "Honestly? I don't know. A guy appeared—a sorcerer, I guess—and shielded us. Thomas was too far away. I don't know how the guy knew it was coming or who he was. He wore a Saints hoodie."

The other man shrugged and shook his head. "Him and everyone else. Why did Lorenzo wait until you were outside to attack?"

"Scott has this building shielded." Lexi rubbed her face. "Can you check that the others got home safely? Then, we need to speak to Joseph."

The door opened and Scott entered. He walked quickly to Lexi. "Are you okay?"

She looked at her feet, swamped by a feeling of failure. "Lorenzo killed Thomas."

He sighed. "I felt you were angry."

"It was nothing." She looked away and her face colored.

Dick raised an eyebrow. "I think we all felt she was angry when she blew the front door off its hinges."

"I didn't hear anything. I only just got back." Scott backed out of the room and returned a minute later. "The door's fixed."

Lexi sat heavily. "Okay, where are we?"

Broullard pocketed his cell. "Everyone made it safely home."

The vampire retrieved a glass. "What the hell are we going to do?"

She was at a loss. "We'll have to try to approach the clan without him."

"What about this other sorcerer? Are Kindred back?" the detective asked.

The question went unanswered as she thought through their options. "Okay, change of plan." She stood, took the key from her pocket, and held it up to Scott. "At first light, we go to see what this unlocks. If Kindred is back in town, I'll have to see them."

Dick poured a large drink for himself. "What if it's the other you?"

Lexi exhaled impatiently. "Honestly, I don't know. But I don't think they're all in on Caleb's plan."

He laughed without humor. "How can you be sure of that?"

She pushed her irritation aside and explained. "When the chief thought he was talking to Alice, he didn't speak to her as though she knew what was going on. He also explicitly told her to keep out of sight but wouldn't say why."

Absently, she turned the key in her hand. *Am I really about to meet my doppelgänger?*

CHAPTER TWENTY

"Are you kidding me?" Lexi stared at Scott.

He held the key and looked at the door in front of them. "Apparently not."

"They live on the same block?" She ended the sentence on a squeak.

The two of them had set out after first light. The key had led them first to the left. Then left at the corner and left again at the next. She took it from Scott. "Is anyone in there?"

His face strained with the effort. "I can't tell. There's a strong shielding spell on the building." He thought for a moment. "You give it a try."

She barked a laugh. "If you can't get through that, what's the point in me trying?"

"Come on—reach out and see what you get."

Lexi closed her eyes and placed her hand over the scar.

"It's empty. How could you not see that?"

"I think your doppelgänger *does* live there. The protections on the house let *you* through but not me."

"Great." She sighed. "That puts you on lookout duty."

She stepped to the door with the key in hand. It swung open

before she had a chance to use it and she looked at Scott and held the key up. "So, what was the point of this?" She turned to the open door and entered.

The house was still. The first floor held a business, with its entrance from the street. This hallway led directly to a stairway and the second floor. She climbed the stairs, entered a sparsely decorated living room, and froze when she glanced at a photograph on the wall. It could have been a picture of herself if she had ever worn a police uniform. Once again, the doppelgänger stood with the same man as in the other photo. They were both in uniform. The woman's face, while identical to Lexi's, did things hers never did—smiling broadly and openly. It was disconcerting.

She glanced into the kitchen, where two cups and plates lay in the sink. Following the hallway to a bathroom, she noted men's and women's products on the shelf.

Okay, so she doesn't live alone. Does she live with her blood match? Does she even have a blood match? She made a mental note to ask Broullard.

In the bedroom, a photograph drew her eye once again. It looked exactly like she might have looked in her early twenties if she had ever worn a wedding gown. The groom's face was obscured by the veil and a thousand pieces of confetti frozen in the air.

Lexi gazed at the bride who seemed so in love and so happy. She wanted to smash her face in. She felt like this creature—this unnatural doppelgänger—had somehow stolen her life.

The front door opened and closed downstairs. Someone was home. Her gaze darted around but there was no exit.

Quickly, she moved to the doorway of the bedroom but the top of someone's head was already visible on the stairs.

She had no choice but to retreat into the bedroom and step into a cupboard with louver doors. The coat hangers were effectively stilled with an arm and she tried not to breathe. A figure moved around outside the cupboard. Through the slats on the door, she could see a pair of men's boots walking around the room. They stopped at the cupboard door and steam rose to her nose, accompanied by a smell of cinnamon. He held a cup of spiced latte and his other hand grasped the cupboard handle. She slipped her hand into her pocket to slide a blade out and her vision blurred. It took a moment to realize she was somewhere else.

Horrified, she spun and gaped at the giant creatures that surrounded and loomed over her. One was directly above. In a flash, the katana was in her hand. She lashed out at the monster closest to her. The blade burst through its skin and hit something hard—bone?

"How cool is this?"

When she whirled again at the loud voice, an avalanche of hard, white balls struck her and flung her off her feet.

"What have you done?" Scott screeched.

Lexi staggered to her feet. "What is that? Where the hell are we?"

He sighed. "We're in my dimensional pocket."

Irritated now, she kicked the balls out of her path. "And what is that?" She pointed at the oddly slumped creature and realized they were everywhere.

His face colored. "It's a Taco Bell chihuahua. I collect them. I just bought that one from a guy a couple of days ago. It was the only one missing from my collection and you killed it."

"I thought it would eat me. How are we here?" Still a little dizzy, she sat on the floor and picked up one of the white beads that was currently the size of a basketball.

The sorcerer pulled the bag from his back and sat beside her. "A guy turned up at the house. I couldn't get past the shield to get you out but your dimensional pocket is linked to mine, so I pulled you out that way."

She looked at the canvas bag. "Hey, wait. Your dimensional pocket is inside that bag."

"Yes."

"So…" She threw the ball aside and dragged the bag into her lap. "Inside this bag, in my hands, is a dimensional pocket with us inside it."

"I guess."

"And there's a bag in there, and inside *that,* is a dimensional pocket with us inside it. Man, that is so fucked up."

Scott took his bag. "It's the same dimensional pocket. There's only one of us."

Her face turned sour, having been reminded of the doppelgänger. "Speak for yourself."

He stood and held his hand out. "Let's get out of here before you have an existential crisis."

"Can we not go anywhere yet?" She placed a ball behind her neck and lay down to stare at the giant toys.

The sorcerer muttered a word and the balls rolled back to the split in the fabric. "What's up? Did the mage see you?"

Lexi felt the tug of the ball at her neck. She sat and it rolled with the others. "No. I don't think so. Uh…so it *was* a mage."

"Definitely. And fairly powerful too from what I could tell. He could sense me too, even though I was shielded. Did you learn anything?"

"She's a cop. You'd think Broullard would have mentioned that. And she's married."

Scott didn't respond. She assumed he would be navigating her conflicted emotions.

Good luck with that.

She watched as he sealed the rip she'd made in the toy. "Scott, what if I am the doppelgänger?"

He lowered his hand and turned to her. "Joseph said you're not."

"Would he even know? I have no real memories of childhood.

I could quite easily have simply appeared one day. My whole life was about being a legacy and working for Kindred. Now, it's all about working for Dolores. This Alice has a career and a husband. There were two cups in the sink and two toothbrushes."

"You feel like she's stolen your life." He held his hand out.

Lexi took it and pushed to her feet. They were back on the street. She turned to the house and looked at the windows. A shadow shifted at one of them. "Let's go."

They didn't speak again until they had turned the corner.

Scott turned to her. "I feel like we're missing something. Why did they create her?"

"Maybe they fixed in her what they couldn't fix in me." She shrugged. Talking about this made her feel exposed and she didn't like it. It was time to change the subject. "I'm sorry I broke your toy."

He rolled his eyes. "They're collectibles."

"Right. I'm sorry I broke your collectible toy." She smirked.

As they entered their building, he paused and pointed up. Someone was up there. He mouthed, "Broullard." They continued to where he leaned against the wall.

Lexi nodded at him. "I thought you'd have been at the other end of the country by now."

He straightened quickly. "I sent my wife to stay at her mother's, but I have some news."

She sniffed the air and smelled cinnamon—exactly the same as in the mage's house—and was immediately on the alert.

Habit kicked in and she stepped ahead. "Me first." She moved forward to check the apartment.

Scott smiled at the other man. "Have you been waiting long?"

"Only a couple of minutes. I thought you were in. It smells like Betsy's been baking pastries. Is she back?"

"Hmm!" Lexi frowned, looked around, then glanced at Broullard "Back? Oh, Betsy, no. She's not back. You had news?"

He sat on a stool at the counter. "The shifters are gearing up to attack Lorenzo's clan."

The sorcerer gaped at him. "Do they know what Lorenzo did to Thomas and his entire clan?"

"They do, but you know what shifters are like. It's all 'I'm more alpha than you are' with them." Broullard shook his head.

Lexi's gaze studied him. He looked uncomfortable. "I feel like you haven't told us everything."

He sighed. "They're talking about taking Kindred on too."

That brought a scowl of disapproval to her face. "They'll bite off more than they can chew."

Scott exhaled a long sigh. "This is suicide."

She nodded but focused on Broullard. "We need to speak to Joseph."

⸻

The two friends sat with Joseph and Geraldine in the courtyard of the little bar.

"You'll get yourselves killed. You need to give us a chance first." Lexi pleaded with Geraldine.

"A chance to do what?" The shifter shrugged.

She rubbed her face. "Firstly, a chance to think of something."

The woman smiled a cold smile. "We've already thought of something. We'll rip Lorenzo's head off."

"I cannot even begin to explain to you how fast he is. He must be ten times faster than any vamp I've seen in my life. I looked right at Thomas when his head was taken off and I didn't even see Lorenzo. He's that fast."

"Not in the daytime, he's not." Geraldine coughed into a handkerchief and they waited.

Scott stood and walked to a wall of flowers. He leaned into them and breathed deeply. "That's amazing." He sighed, then turned to the others. "We need to get that ring back."

Lexi shook her head. "I don't think either of them is willing to let that happen."

"I might be able to assist with that." A light breeze rippled through the courtyard as Joseph spoke. "My spirits have dominion over the dead, so the dead are mine to command."

She looked at him and quirked an eyebrow. "Could you make him get up in the middle of the day and walk into the sun? Because that would really work for me."

The man drew his mouth down in thought. "Possibly."

Geraldine folded her arms. "What about Kindred? They interfered with the first night of The Shifting. Worse, they plan to murder our children and deserve to be destroyed."

"Something is bad in Kindred. We're looking into it, but we don't know who's involved and who's not." She lifted the coffee in front of her and took a sip. "If the kids have somewhere safe to go, will they still be able to continue tonight?"

"Most of the families observed the first night at home. Tonight is shifting night. How can we ensure our young are safe to shift?"

Scott sat and leaned forward. "I've spoken to Dolores. The fae are offering the Immortal Glades."

The shifter's eyes widened. "I thought the Immortal Glades was a myth. But the fae can be tricksy. How can we be sure the kids will come back?"

He smiled. "You can select a few of the elders to go with them."

"And you." She pointed at him. "I want you with them. I trust you."

The sorcerer shook his head. "But you barely know me."

Geraldine grinned. "I'm a good judge of character."

"We really need to—" he began, still shaking his head

"That's fine," his partner interrupted. "We'll make it work."

The shifter nodded her agreement.

Lexi looked around the table. "Great. So, we'll get the kids to safety and Joseph can do his thing with Lorenzo. Does anyone know where he'll be sleeping?"

Joseph nodded. "He lives at the bar."

She turned to Scott. "Can you sort out the details with Dolores and Geraldine? If this doesn't work, you'll need to get the kids to safety. I'll see you across the street from Lorenzo's bar in an hour."

He nodded. They walked away from the others and although he didn't look happy, he took her hand and transferred magic to her. "We only transferred this morning and you're almost empty again. It's getting worse. We shouldn't be apart."

The magic drained remarkably fast, something she'd noticed, and it worried her. Still, this wasn't the time to discuss it. "I'll get back to the apartment and let Broullard know what's happening." She turned at the door. "Joseph, do you know where in the bar Lorenzo sleeps?"

"He has an apartment over it but his entire clan has been there for the past few nights. He won't let any of them go home."

"Okay, I'll see you there in an hour." She walked through the bar and out onto the street.

At home again, Lexi took out the key to open the door but was immediately dragged into the opposite apartment by Dick.

She opened her mouth to speak but he made wild helicopter signals with his finger. While she wasn't happy to use the magic, she made it safe to speak. "What's wrong?"

The vampire closed the door and whispered, "You paid you a visit."

"Excuse me?" She narrowed her eyes. "And why are you whispering?"

He continued in a low tone. "Your doppelgänger was here earlier with a tall, dark-haired young man. Very handsome, actually."

"Did she see Broullard?" She glanced instinctively toward her apartment door. "Where is he?"

"He put a note under my door a while ago. He went to check on his wife and will be back soon."

Lexi sighed with relief. "Okay, so I've been to her place and she's been to mine. What did she say?"

"Do you think I'm crazy? I didn't speak to them. I peeked through the peephole in the door and didn't make a sound. She looked exactly like you...well, except for the thighs, obviously. And scars down her face. It looked like she'd been mauled by a bear or a shifter. Maybe a shifter bear." He stopped and thought for a moment. "Would that be a werebear? Anyway, he couldn't get past Scott's shielding but she did. She walked straight in."

"They were in our apartment?"

"Only her and for less than a minute. They were talking when she came out. She said 'There's no way that apartment is being used by Kindred unless Julia Child is a legacy. The place is full of cookies.' Then they walked down the hallway. Where's Scott?"

"He's making arrangements with the shifters and I'll meet him with Joseph at the bar. Hopefully, we can put an end to Lorenzo and Delphine. If that doesn't work, Scott will help to get the shifter kids to Fae tonight."

Dick walked her to the door. "It's so frustrating having to stay out of the way in daylight."

Lexi met with Scott and Joseph across the street from Lorenzo's bar.

She scanned their surroundings in all directions. "Is he in there?"

Scott nodded. "Yes. Well, the ring's in there. Assuming it's still on him, so is he."

The other man began to shake his staff. She hadn't looked properly at it before. The symbols carved into it were unfamiliar to her and bones and shells hung from a fibrous string wound around the top. They made a clattering sound when he shook it.

He stooped and dropped granules of salt or maybe light sand onto the sidewalk in an intricate design. When he spoke, it was in a language that sounded vaguely French but was possibly an African dialect. She raised her eyebrows at Scott.

"Haitian, I think," he whispered.

Joseph continued while the two friends stared at the door of the bar across the street.

The sorcerer stiffened. "The ring's coming closer. I can feel it."

After about a minute, Lexi opened her mouth to ask what was going on when she heard shouts from inside the building across the street. The door opened and several vampires massed in the doorway. The man at the front pushed back against the others and wedged an arm and leg against the frame, while he covered his face from the daylight with his other arm. After a few moments, he was shoved out into the sunlight. He emitted a short scream and burst into flames. It wasn't Lorenzo, though. Several vamps behind him edged—obviously against their will—toward the door, pushed from behind.

She turned to Joseph. "What's happening?"

"I'm pulling him to the door but he's forcing his clan to block his exit. I can continue but he'll push them all out to save himself."

Another vampire, this one a young woman, stood at the edge of the doorway with a look of terror on her face. All she could think of were the parents of the vampire girl Lorenzo had killed. "Stop. Just...stop."

The man stretched his staff out and dragged it through the symbol on the ground. The door across the street slammed.

"Shit!" She punched a wall in utter frustration. "Let's get out of here."

Broullard, Scott, Joseph, and Lexi sat around the table in the apartment.

The detective stood, walked to the window, and looked onto the street. "The only people equipped to deal with this are Kindred, and they're the ones behind it."

Scott looked at the time. "We need to start moving those kids to Fae. Hopefully, Lorenzo will spend the night running around the bayou looking for them."

Joseph shook his head. "He'll know instantly by the smell that they're not there."

The sorcerer folded his arms and pushed his bottom lip out, his expression thoughtful. "Maybe."

Broullard looked at him. "What are you thinking?"

He smiled. "I can leave a wolf-scented trail through the least populated parts of the bayou. It should keep him busy for a while."

The man looked doubtful. "But he moves so fast."

Lexi leaned forward and took one of Betsy's cookies from a tub in the middle of the table. She grinned. "He can't move faster than his boat." She pushed the bowl to Scott. "That deserves a cookie."

CHAPTER TWENTY-ONE

Dolores, Scott, and George arrived at a small jetty in the bayou, twenty miles out from the city.

The sorcerer looked at Agatha's father. "Are you ready?"

He nodded "Ready when you are."

They climbed aboard the boat and set off. George sat at the outboard motor and steered the craft through the bayou, deserted by all life beyond gators and bugs.

Scott worked his magic as they moved through narrow channels and paused to climb onto dry land and push through tendrils of Spanish moss dangling from the limbs of trees.

They climbed aboard the boat and continued the journey.

Dolores twisted to face the shifter. "Can you tell me about the shifting ritual?"

"On the first night, the children gather with their parents, older siblings, or other elders. We spend the evening around campfires in the bayou. The older ones tell stories—old stories, the passing on of knowledge—and tell them their own stories."

The sorcerer looked curiously at him. "Their own stories?"

George nodded. "About their first shift, however many years ago that was. The second night, the kids shift. They feel the moonlight for the first time and run. After that, they can shift anytime. Those who get the curse—the ones who shift because they are bitten—can only turn on the full moon or the command of their sire. They are not shifters and are what we call werewolves."

The others already knew this but both nodded politely.

"What happens on the third night?" Dolores asked.

"The new shifters tell their story and they repeat the old stories back to us. Usually, they shift a few more times too, merely because they can. We run as a family. We'll run with Agatha tomorrow night, I hope."

For several hours, they laid a trail around the bayou over miles of wetland. Scott carefully increased the scent as they moved, giving the impression that the shifters were closer together.

"I've done everything I can. It's almost sundown. Let's get to Fae."

On land, Dolores summoned the fae door and stepped aside for them. The shifter hesitated and peered through to a forest path that opened into a grassy glade.

Scott tapped his shoulder. "Or you can stay here and wait for Lorenzo."

George turned to him. "Have you been over there?"

He grinned. "Nope. This is my first time and the anticipation is killing me." They stepped through.

When they reached the clearing, Agatha ran to her father and hugged him. "Dad, there were fae people here and some of them were flying." She caught his hand and pulled him along the edge of the glade to the base of polished wooden stairs that led to platforms in the trees. They ascended to find nine youngsters and twenty adults seated there with cups and plates, laughing and joking.

"How's Marcel, Agatha?" Scott asked.

She grinned. "He's great. I looked after him good. Mom

couldn't come because she has to look after Anton, so she's watching Marcel too."

A girl of about sixteen in a pair of denim shorts and a strappy top that revealed her midriff jumped up as they approached. "You sit here, Dad." She spoke to George but she gazed at Scott in a way that made him feel uncomfortable.

The shifter nodded to the other parents before he sat and put his arm around Agatha. The sorcerer sat on a tree branch that extended a foot higher than the platform they were on. Immediately, the young shifter woman sat beside him, closer than he felt was appropriate.

"We've learned about the first shifters, and Grandpa told me about when he shifted for the first time out in the bayou and he ate a raccoon—can you believe that?" Agatha pretended to throw up.

George laughed. "He told me that story too, Nugget." He mussed his young daughter's hair.

She straightened and finger-combed it. "Tell me about your first shift."

He flicked an uncomfortable glance at Scott and Dolores.

"I have work to do," the fae announced.

"I'll help." Scott attempted to rise but the young woman curled her arm around his.

She turned to George. "Scott doesn't need to go anywhere, does he?"

The shifter shook his head. "Of course not. Scott, you're welcome to listen. But Gretchen, don't you make a nuisance of yourself."

The girl released his arm but tutted and rolled her eyes.

He tried to concentrate on the tale but he worried about how Lexi was doing without him. They'd agreed that she and Dick would stay in the apartments unless needed. She was a world away, but he could still feel her emotional state. She was pensive. Although, he reminded himself, she was always pensive, so that was a good thing. He came out of his reverie when Gretchen put her hand on his knee.

He stared at the hand and into her face. Her lips twitched. He looked at George who was finishing his tale. "And that's what a muskrat tastes like."

"Daddy, you didn't." Agatha was horrified.

Something tickled Scott's head and he patted his hair. Finding nothing, he lowered his arm and tried to think of a way to get the girl's hand off his knee without offending her.

The shifters began to look at the moon.

"It's almost time." George looked into the sky, and the youngsters stood to make their way down the steps.

"Remember what you've been told." Dolores' voice came from below. "You mustn't travel beyond this forest. I've secured safe passage for the pack in this forest and glade only. This isn't your world and to put it bluntly, humans are not the top of the food chain here. Neither are shifters."

Scott felt another tickle and slapped the back of his neck quickly. Something crawled down the back of his t-shirt. He leapt to his feet, yanked his shirt out, and searched down his back with one hand and up with the other. Gretchen moved away from him. The remaining adult shifters stared at him as though he had gone crazy.

As the crawling sensation moved to his side, tickling him, he fought a manic giggle. He pictured a spider or scorpion and hopped frantically before he finally pulled his t-shirt off. It was on his stomach. He swept his hand to flick the tiny winged creature off as it seemed to be making its way into his pants. It spun away and landed on a branch, and he squinted to see it better from where he stood, breathing heavily.

"What the hell is that?"

Gretchen addressed his abs, "Did it bite you?"

He held his t-shirt up to cover himself in front of the girl, who looked much too appreciative.

His gaze remained fixed on the creature as it began to grow.

It slowly became larger and was clearly not an insect. A fully formed and very beautiful young fae woman sat on the branch and studied him.

Her eyes sparkled. "Well, that was quite a ride. Do you want to go again?" She tilted her head and smiled.

He stared open-mouthed at the scantily clad fairy. Her shiny auburn hair hung over her shoulder like satin, her lips were large, and her eyes smoldered with an intense dark-brown. As if that wasn't enough to befuddle his brain, her clothes were just the wrong side of decent.

"Do you like what you see?" She winked.

"Aleena!" Dolores stood on the platform. "The forest and glade are off-limits to fae tonight."

Scott jumped at the woman's voice and replaced his t-shirt quickly.

Aleena kept her gaze on him. "I'm going."

A low growl issued from beside Scott. He turned to see Gretchen's golden wolf-eyes fixed on the fae woman.

"Gretchen!" George admonished the girl. The fairy glanced at her, giggled, held her arms out to her sides, and fell back off the platform.

The sorcerer gasped and stepped to the edge, but she skimmed the long grass of the glade gracefully with almost no movement to her wings. She floated upright at the edge of the forest and gave him a little finger wave before she vanished.

Gretchen stepped beside him, her face like stone. "With a little luck, she'll hang around and Agatha will bite her wings off. That'll make a better story than a muskrat."

Scott turned to Dolores. His brows were drawn in thought. "Can you fly?"

She looked at him as though he'd lost his mind. "Of course I can." She looked into the forest where Aleena had disappeared. "I probably shouldn't have let you come. This could be a problem."

He bristled. "I'm not interested."

"It's not always optional with some of my kind. Be careful while you're here."

"I can look after myself." He knew he had begun to sound sulky.

Dolores patted his arm. "Of course you can, dear. But don't speak to anyone."

Gretchen slipped her arm through his. "I'll look after him."

"You'll do no such thing, young lady." George curled his finger to her. "You come and sit with me until they get back."

She complied and went to sit with her father but wouldn't release Scott. He was forced to sit there too and blushed furiously.

CHAPTER TWENTY-TWO

Lorenzo awoke. He breathed in, assessed the taste and smell of his surroundings, and concluded that nothing was amiss.

About time. Delphine's voice sounded snippy in his mind.

He made a mental eye-roll and wondered if the enhanced abilities were worth the exhaustion from this psychopathic harridan who lived in his mind. She didn't ever seem to shut up. Worse, the compulsion to follow her every whim made it a constant battle to not give in to her desires. Her life-force was incredibly strong, more than when he first wore the ring. It had taken considerable time to control her but now, it seemed to have become harder.

Draining the tourists in the courtyard directly after he put the ring on had been the result of her inability to control the blood-lust. It was inconvenient, but they had come to an agreement. He allowed her entertainments and she gave him extraordinary speed and strength. In his quiet moments, he still couldn't believe he'd eliminated Thomas' entire coven on his own. They hadn't known what hit them. His lips twitched as he lay there and recalled what Delphine had done to Thomas. It had been a disgusting display and quite distasteful but he had been a sancti-monious prick, after all.

His thoughts turned to Joseph. Now *he* was a disappointment. Lorenzo had always respected him and even liked him. But he couldn't go unpunished, not after he pulled his voodoo shit.

This caused a problem, though. He needed Joseph to help him get this fucking woman out of his head without losing the abilities the ring gave him.

Well? Do you intend to move?

Without thought, he stretched to touch the metal lid above him. He snatched his hand away. She'd made him reach out like that and he decided she could damn well wait.

The absolute shame and embarrassment of his present situation were that he was forced to sleep in a metal box in case Joseph tried something again. He inwardly groaned at the thought.

The box was useful for another reason, however. He was aware that Delphine had moved in his body while he was asleep. At least she couldn't get out in the daytime, but he had woken the night before with his silver-tipped dagger in hand as he stood over Darnell, one of his most trusted clan members.

Of course, he knew about Delphine LaLaurie. Almost everyone who lived in or visited the French Quarter knew about her, but he wondered why the mad bitch had such a problem with black people.

"It's time to visit the bayou. I promised to reduce the shifter numbers."

Who cares what you promised?

"I like to think of myself as a man of my word." He thumped the lid.

The box opened from the outside and Darnell waited next to it.

Lorenzo stood and stepped out of the metal box. "Any news?"

The other man closed the box once his leader had taken a couple of steps away from it. "The donors are here."

Ahh, breakfast! Delphine's desire for blood raised his anticipation. His teeth descended.

He closed his mouth and mentally reasserted control over himself. His gaze located a familiar donor, although he didn't know her name. "Well?"

She approached and held her arm out.

Lorenzo rolled his eyes. "I want information. Did you do what you were told?"

"Yes. The shifters were seen heading to the bayou a couple of hours ago. I watched Joseph. He went to one of Oberon's guest apartments but I don't know why—"

He cut her off. "That's okay. I can guess who he's with. I think I'll have to speak to Oberon about the company he keeps." He turned to Darnell. "Keep Joseph's serviteurs busy until I get back but I want Joseph alive."

The donor remained and offered her arm again.

"You can go. I'll eat out tonight." He smiled when he felt Delphine's disappointment.

———

A little later, Lorenzo parked his Porsche nine-eleven on the gravel beside the jetty. This was the second location he'd stopped at. The shifters didn't always use the same place for their ritual but he knew this was the right one. It stank of wolf, which was a good sign. He looked at the available craft moored along the waterside. The giant tour boat was no good as it was too large. The airboat would be too loud. That left the small boat with an outboard motor in front of him. He untied the line, dropped into it, and looked around for a potential owner. There was no doubt that he was alone so he shrugged and started the motor.

The boat moved slowly through the water and he followed

the scent of the wolves and branched off into smaller, narrower water lanes. The smells intensified. Moving at this speed was frustrating, but he couldn't afford to miss a potential victim. He was supposed to kill a handful of them. That's what he'd agreed but he was powerful now. He intended to obliterate the pack's future generations and couldn't wait to find the newly turned shifter kids. Neither, he sensed, could Delphine.

After they'd returned to the boat for the third time, he began to wonder where in hell they all were. Every time he thought he was close, he would find himself on an island with nothing but cypress trees for company.

"Finally!" he muttered to himself after more than an hour. He approached a small jetty, which led to a cabin.

A fire-pit burned outside, and the windows glowed with light. The smell of wolf was heavy in the air. He cut the motor and drifted to the shore. With the motor off, he could hear low, muttered voices from inside the cabin. He deduced they'd finished their shifting and were all inside, so he tied the boat off and stepped onto land. Knowing how keen the wolves' hearing was, he guessed they would already know someone was there. In mere seconds, they would catch the scent of a vampire. Sadly for them, they didn't have seconds.

With his improved speed, he hurtled around the cabin to the door and burst through immediately, only to find it completely empty. He walked to the center of the room, a little confused as he knew he'd heard people. Suddenly, flames flared all around him and seemed to fill the cabin. Within a second, he was outside. He checked his clothes for fire damage, stepped away from the building, and scowled as the blaze incinerated it.

Oh dear. You've been tricked. Delphine laughed, but Lorenzo could tell she was angry too.

He walked around the cabin to find the little boat but it floated beyond reach and it too was engulfed in flames. "Whoever did this, I'll tear them to shreds."

Oberon huffed as he lifted the crate of empty beer bottles into the dumpster behind the bar.

"You must be Oberon." He jumped, startled. The voice was male but it sounded quite soft.

He spun, puzzled, and looked around for someone else. "Lorenzo—" The words cut off when he was held by the throat against the edge of the dumpster.

"I'd like a little chat about who you've rented your guest apartments to lately." The vampire had taken control of the conversation.

The sanguinaire tried to answer but his larynx was being crushed.

"Obe?" Martine stepped out and froze at the back door of the bar.

Before she could react, his captor had dropped him and held her by the hair in front of him.

"Your friend here would like you to answer us."

"Us?" His gaze scanned the area and returned to the vampire. "It's someone called Dick. He's here with friends."

Lorenzo remembered the apartment across from William's. When the Kindred bitch had told him William was off-limits, it hadn't taken him long to learn that the vampire had a puppy. He'd gone there to snap the scrawny little mutt's neck. As soon as he had left the staircase, he'd felt drawn to the other apartment. He could smell the dog but something seductive had drawn him to that apartment. The stunning woman who had answered the door had assumed he was Peter, a friend of someone called Dick.

Peter, of course, was the name of the guy they'd poisoned to get to William, so that couldn't be a coincidence. Was Dick a friend of William's?

He had decided in that moment to forget the dog. Instead,

he'd intended to murder the woman if she had the slightest connection to his adversary.

Delphine interrupted his thoughts. *I could have told you his name is Dick. I stabbed him with a silver blade.*

Martine squealed. "He has another name—William."

"Oberon. Did you try to lie to me?" The entity within him spoke now. Lorenzo had opened his mouth to speak and her voice came out. She had become even stronger and without warning, she spun Martine and drove her head into a wall. With their combined strength, that was all it took to reduce her skull to a bloody, dripping pulp. The body fell and Delphine released the piece of hair and scalp still in his hand. "Now, what is William up to?"

The vampire forced himself to regain control of his own body. "So, William's still in town. Interesting." He was about to finish Oberon when a globe the size of a basketball floated into view. It was high and very bright.

"What the—" He stared at it as it began to pulse and glow brighter and after a few seconds, he had to avert his eyes. Suddenly, it blasted light and it was like staring at the sun. Lorenzo shrieked as the light scorched his eyes and skin. He covered his face with his arm before he disappeared in the opposite direction.

CHAPTER TWENTY-THREE

Agatha padded through the forest. She had been running and the breeze through her fur had been exhilarating. Beneath her excitement, she was aware of the edges of the mental link with her pack and knew it would strengthen over the next few hours. She stopped to sniff at the undergrowth. Every new scent was like a story in her mind, the passage of creatures, what direction they had traveled in, how many, and how long they had stayed. In some cases, she could picture the animal simply by its smell. Others were a mystery, no doubt denizens of this strange, beautiful world.

The edge of the forest opened before her. A dirt track ran along the edge and she wondered if it circled the whole woodland area. The moon reflected upon a beautiful lake before her on the other side of the track. She knew she shouldn't leave the trees, but this was a perfect opportunity to see her reflection and to look upon herself as a wolf for the very first time. She sniffed the air, listened to the silence, and looked up and down the track. Tentatively, she stepped out and made her way across it to the water.

Standing at the edge, she looked at her reflection. She had

already seen that her fur was black at the roots and turned to a reddish-brown at the ends but now, she could see that around her snout and cheeks, it was white, exactly like her mother and older sister, Gretchen.

Oh, my God. I'm a white girl. It was hilarious. She laughed and it sounded unnatural coming from a wolf.

Ripples flowed through her reflection and distorted it as though something had moved in the water. Her ears pricked and she took a step back, ready to return to the forest. As she glanced across the water, she saw the reflection of another white face. She looked up at a beautiful horse that stood motionless in the reeds. When she focused on it, the animal whinnied and shook. She remembered she was a wolf.

The poor guy must be terrified.

She shifted to human form and walked around the edge of the lake to the horse.

"It's okay. See? I'm only a person." Agatha could see it wore a bridle but no saddle. She held her hand out slowly. The horse backed away from the water's edge and stepped tentatively toward her. It nuzzled her hand, then allowed her to stroke its flank.

The girl muttered softly as she stroked it. "You're the most beautiful thing I've ever seen. I wish I had an apple for you. You look as beautiful as a unicorn."

Before her eyes, a horn appeared in the middle of the creature's head. It was white and pearlescent. Her heart exploded with love. She looked around and wished one of the others could come out of the forest so she could share the experience, but she and the unicorn were alone.

"So, you shift too. Are unicorns shifters?" She wondered how many of the horses she'd seen on earth were unicorns in disguise.

The creature shook its head so its long mane fell to the side, and she stroked it. It shook its head again and this time, tilted its head toward her. Was it an invitation?

"Do you want me to ride you?" Agatha couldn't quite believe it.

When the unicorn did it a third time, she didn't need to be asked again. She wound her fingers into its mane and, using her shifter strength and agility, vaulted onto its back. It surprised her how comfortable she felt, and she looked around again, hoping one of the others might still appear and capture the moment with their cellphone.

What a profile pic this would make.

"I wonder if I could ride you into the forest. I'm sure none of my friends would eat a unicorn." She'd never ridden a horse in her life and tried leaning in the direction of the track to encourage it in that direction. It stood unmoving. "Giddy-up?" she asked hopefully.

The animal took a step forward.

"Well, that's something but not the right direction." She pointed. "We want to go that way."

Another step toward the water made her deduce that it probably wanted a drink. "Okay, you get a drink as long as I don't fall off." She looked at the ground and now realized how high she was. The shift was making her bones stronger but that fall would still hurt, and there was no Lexi to catch her with magic this time.

The creature took two more steps and its front legs were in the water, but it didn't seem to be drinking.

"I'm gonna be honest. This is turning into a disappointment." Agatha decided it was time to dismount.

She tried to lift her leg over so she could drop off, but the limb wouldn't move. It was stuck. Confused, she attempted to lift her other leg, but that was stuck too. She decided to try to pull her leg up with her hands but she couldn't shake its mane from her fingers. Alarmed now, she pressed her hands down to lever herself up, but her body was stuck solidly to the unicorn. When she tried to pull her hands free, they wouldn't move.

As she watched, the unicorn's horn blackened from its tip and dissolved into nothing. The creature's body slowly darkened to black to reveal an ugly horse-like creature. It flicked its head and looked disdainfully at her with red eyes, while its jaws snapped and showed sharp, pointed teeth.

Agatha shrieked into the forest "Help. Help me." She screamed and thrashed frantically as it stepped further into the water.

Her gaze locked on a beautiful fairy seated in a tree above her. Her head was tilted and her brow drawn with curiosity as she stared at the little girl's predicament.

"Help me, please. I can't get off."

The fairy stared a moment longer, then rolled her eyes and flew into the forest.

"Don't leave me, please," the girl cried, and the creature took another step. It seemed to delight in drawing her terror out.

Scott pulled a tub of cookies from his bag and passed them around the group.

Dolores looked at them. "Betsy's?"

He nodded. "Is she still here? How's Todd?"

"They're here, staying in my cottage. He's ready to go home but now we know Caleb's still alive and a threat to them, they'll stay a little longer. We really must resolve that issue."

The sorcerer nodded his agreement. "How will we find Caleb?"

"If that demon is with him, it must still be trying to escape to this earth. The hell dimension he was in when we last encountered him is of no use to him now. I have someone trying to find other possible points of intersection—" Dolores stopped speaking and stared into the distance.

Scott followed her gaze and noticed Aleena, the young fae woman, returning at speed.

She drew to a halt in the branches of the tree. "A kelpie has one of the pups."

As one, the adults stood.

"What's a kelpie?"

"Who has it got?"

"Where?"

Aleena pointed at Gretchen. "The one that smells like her."

Wings unfurled from Dolores's back. Her skirt suit was gone and so was her middle-aged visage. "You all wait here." She swooped away toward the tree line.

"The hell I will." Gretchen shifted and bounded to the ground from their platform.

Scott expected her father to call her back but they all shifted and followed. He wanted to as well but knew his boss would expect him to obey her orders.

"Alone at last." Aleena wiggled her eyebrows.

He ignored her and began to pace.

She sat on the branch, watched him, and began to sing quietly in a language he didn't understand.

Dolores burst from the forest to the edge of the lake. A moment later, she was joined by the shifters, who barked and growled at the edge of the water. They could smell the girl's trail and knew where she was.

The surface, however, was still.

The fae hovered over it before she plunged in. She found them a few feet down. Agatha was still on the creature's back but was beginning to unstick. Her hands had loosened and drifted limply in the water.

She surged out of the water. "I found them. She's still stuck to its back, though. If I try to pull her off, the kelpie will strengthen its hold on her and disappear into the depths. I have to grab the bridle. It's the only way to control the beast."

Without waiting for a response, she submerged again. The creature had begun to move. It became aware of her before she could get close and began to thrash its head in an attempt to prevent her from taking hold of the bridle. Its head met hers and shoved her back.

If this thing knocks me out, I'm no good to the girl.

She glanced to where George and Gretchen swam down. Each took one of Agatha's hands. It was now or never.

Dolores swam in quickly, aided by her wings, and ignored the creature's thrashing and attempts to bite her. She grasped the bridle and commanded her intent with her mind as she stared into the beast's eyes.

Let her go.

The kelpie had no choice but to submit. The sticky surface on its back dissolved and Agatha floated free. George and Gretchen swam with her to the surface. The fae kept hold of the bridle until they were out, then she released and rocketed to the surface. It snapped at her feet as it followed.

She hovered above the water for a moment and flapped the water out of her wings. Caution pushed through and she moved higher a second before the kelpie's head thrust from the water with a snap of its pointed teeth. It splashed into the lake and sank into the depths.

Quickly, she flew to where George blew into Agatha's lungs. There was no response.

Dolores made a fae door. "Let's get her to Scott."

The shifter sat back, exhausted. Another lifted the girl's limp, unresponsive body and a couple of the others helped her father. They walked through the door and onto the platform.

Scott sat on the branch, glassy-eyed, and smiled at them while rivulets of blood ran into his t-shirt. Aleena sat on his lap and feasted on his neck. In two seconds, all the shifters except the one holding Agatha had shifted and circled her with warning growls.

The fae stopped, looked at them, then turned her face to Scott. She fixed her gaze on them and made one long lick up the length of his neck.

Dolores was furious. "Release him."

Aleena smiled and rubbed blood from his lips, then her own. "You know that's not how it works, Dolores. He's mine now."

The wolves snarled and moved closer.

After a glance at Agatha's lifeless form, the young fae rolled her eyes and stood. "Fine. But only temporarily."

Scott shook his head in surprise at the wolves surrounding him. "What's going on?"

The man holding Agatha stepped forward. "She needs your aid."

He helped him lay her down and put a hand over her eyes.

"No." Gretchen's hand flew to her mouth. The wolves still around Aleena whined.

Dolores calmed them. "It's okay. He's only reading her."

The sorcerer nodded. He placed his hand over the bottom of her ribs and muttered.

"I don't understand. It's not working. What's happened to my magic?"

Aleena shrugged and smirked. "Oopsie."

Dolores gave her a withering look. She thrust a handful of stones into his hand and he held them in his fist and drew the magic in.

He began again and nothing happened for a few moments, then water gushed from Agatha's mouth. She gulped air, convulsed, and threw up more liquid. Her eyes fluttered open and her father pulled her into his arms and wept.

A shifter woman sighed. "Why would she go near a creature like that in the first place? Much less climb upon it's back?"

Aleena snorted. "She thought it was a unicorn. It even produced a horn to encourage her to climb up."

George stared at her. "You were there before the kelpie ensnared her. You could have stopped this."

The shifters moved toward the fae.

Scott wobbled, still drawing the last of the magic from the stones into him. He began to feel it again in the air and drew on that too. After a few moments, he sat bolt upright. "Something's wrong with Lexi."

"Okay, you go. I'll get the others home." Dolores called her fae door again as he picked his bag up."

"I don't think so." The young fae crooked her finger at him. He dropped the bag immediately and walked to her.

She looked at the shifters. "His blood is in my heart and mine is in his. If you kill me, you kill him."

Dolores looked meaningfully at Gretchen and drew the young sorcerer's attention. "Scott, you need to return to Lexi."

While his focus was diverted, Gretchen stepped beside Aleena and swung her fist so hard into her face, the fae was unconscious before she landed.

"Damn, that felt good." The shifter shook her hand out.

Scott shook his head and gaped at the unconscious fae girl. "What's going on here? What does she keep doing to me?"

His boss picked his bag up and pushed it into his hands. "She's Dearg-Due, a form of dark fae. She mesmerized you. It'll leave you feeling a little uncomfortable for a while. She won't be a problem soon as she'll be in a cell in The Hollows within the hour."

"What kind of uncomfortable?" He looked nervous.

"You'll…uh, pine for her." She stepped to Aleena, stooped, and poked her in the forehead. The unconscious fae shrank to the size of a wasp. Dolores produced a little bottle from her pocket, pulled the stopper out, and dropped the diminutive creature into it before she secured it and slipped it into her pocket.

"I need to get to Lexi." Scott moved to the door.

Half of the shifters lined up behind him. George patted him on the back. "Whatever's going on, you won't face it alone."

While the remaining shifters waited with Dolores, Gretchen, and Agatha for the rest of the kids to return, Scott and the others stepped through the doorway.

CHAPTER TWENTY-FOUR

Lexi looked at the fae door and sighed with relief when Scott walked through with the shifters. Immediately, she began to draw magic from him. They were in the scented courtyard at the back of the tiny bar where they had met Joseph. She was on her knees and held her hand over a bloody, ragged tear in a man's neck. He gasped when he realized she was covered in blood.

"It's not mine. Well, most of it isn't. Can you help this guy?" She moved aside to allow him to close the wound. It had closed halfway, then stopped responding. The wound lay half-open and blood dribbled out slowly.

The sorcerer shook his head. "I'm losing him." He put his hands over the man's heart and head. "What happened?" He muttered his spells.

"It was Lorenzo's clan. They began to attack about an hour ago. I was with Joseph when he got the call." She indicated the damaged bodies lying around her. "Most of this happened before we got here. Someone managed to keep them out at first, but no one here was as strong as Joseph. They've attacked every few minutes and it feels like they're playing with us. They seem to know exactly how long it takes Joseph to raise his protection magic. He's exhausted and my magic disappeared in the first five minutes."

Scott looked around. "Where's Dick?"

"He went to get help." She looked soberly at him. "He's been gone a long time."

Joseph came out of the bar with towels and hurried toward the man on the ground next to Lexi. He took in the condition of the body and passed one of the towels to Scott as he gazed around the courtyard. Dried blood encrusted his head and his eyes were slightly unfocused. "They'll be back at any moment. We should—"

Vampires surged over the roof at the rear and dropped into the courtyard. Their faces filled with shock in mid-air when they noticed the pack of wolves that had apparently appeared from nowhere.

"Keep them off me," Scott yelled.

Lexi lurched into action as a man barreled into her with his teeth bared. His movements were a blur, but it was nowhere near her first fight with a vampire. She had neither the time nor the space to draw her katana, but she used his momentum against him, spun him easily, and yanked a button from her vest. It came away with a length of silver wire at the back of it which she flicked deftly around the vampire's neck. He tried to right his balance but she shoved him away with her foot and hauled hard on the wire to sever his head. As he fell, she drew her katana and finished the next one with a deft sweep.

Pain flared in her arm as glass shattered against it. She looked up and scowled when she realized it had been thrown by the female vampire who had been close to meeting the sun earlier that day in the failed plan to eliminate Lorenzo and Delphine. The others were almost all gone. She and the man beside her were the last and it was a desperate move by a vampire surrounded by wolves. They descended on her. Lexi glowered at the cut on her arm and the blood that trickled visibly.

No good deed ever goes unpunished.

The vampire woman and her friend were savaged moments later by the wolves.

She felt a wave of sadness and turned to Scott, who placed the blood-soaked towel over the face of the guy he'd tried to save.

Lexi glanced at the glass doors to the bar. "We need to get inside. Let's move the bodies in."

Joseph shook his head. He looked sad and weary. "Leave them. Their work is not done." They entered the building and the man closed the glass doors and began to pour sand on the floor.

Scott extended his arms to the doors with his palms out and muttered a few words. A bluish light flowed across the apertures, then vanished. "We're protected."

He put a hand over her cut arm. While he healed her, he looked at the worried faces in the bar. His gaze fell on two people slumped over a table in the corner. "Are they—"

She shook her head. "No, they're tourists. Joseph thought it would be better if they slept through this."

A moment later, he tapped her arm to indicate he'd finished healing her. "Why hasn't he controlled the vamps like he did before?"

Lexi looked at the healed wound and nodded her thanks. "They're starting too far away, and they're in and out before he can get a mental grip on them."

The sorcerer studied Joseph's remaining people. "Couldn't the serviteurs help?"

"They're busy keeping the vamps away from the front of the building and look at them—they're almost wiped-out."

He glanced at those who stood over sand patterns on the floor and tables along the front wall. They did look exhausted.

George left his group of shifters and joined them. "We should be out there." He pointed to the courtyard.

"We need a better plan than wasting your lives to slow them. They'll know the last three they sent didn't come back, and it'll be sun-up in a couple of hours. I think the attacks will get bigger."

The words were barely out of Lexi's mouth when a half-dozen vampires landed in the courtyard. They raced toward the doors but met Scott's shield and fell back. The glass doors vibrated for a couple of seconds, then stilled. The invaders looked at each other before they leapt away and over the low roof at the side of the courtyard.

Scott went to look through the windows on the front of the building. He returned a few minutes later. "Why are they doing this?"

She shrugged. "I'd guess Lorenzo's pissed that Joseph tried to light him up this afternoon."

He raised an eyebrow. "And he'll be very pissed if he followed the trail through the bayou to the end. Anyway, I mean why are they attacking this way? There's enough of them to have stormed in here the moment the sun went down. Is this a distraction? If so, from what?"

Lexi retrieved several shurikens and clipped them to the front of her vest. "You saw what Lorenzo and Delphine did to Thomas. Maybe the plan is to make an example out of Joseph. Or perhaps they're amusing themselves while they wait to see if any shifters return from the bayou."

The sorcerer drew his brows together in thought. "I'm surprised Lorenzo's not back already. I'm sure we led him on a merry trail, but he should have discovered the truth by now."

She looked at a map on the wall. "Could you track the ring with this?"

He seemed to consider it for a moment but finally shook his head. "I could use one that's a little more detailed. The whole of Louisiana's on that."

After a moment's thought, she seemed to have an idea. "But couldn't you see if you can feel the ring close by?"

Scott rolled his eyes. "Yes, of course. I don't know why I didn't think of it." She stared at him. He usually closed his eyes for something like this but this time, he merely stared directly ahead. "He's here."

"What, in town? Can you tell how close?"

"I'd say about twenty feet." He pointed to the courtyard. Lexi turned to see the vampire on the other side of the glass.

Lorenzo stared at her. "You're behind all this? I think you missed a memo. You need to speak to your boss." He stepped forward and swung at the glass. His hand met the shield first but the glass vibrated so much, she thought it would shatter.

Lexi smirked. "I think I'm up to date, thanks. How's your new roomie?"

His voice changed and became softer and higher. "You're looking well since I stabbed you in the gut." His face became furious, then calm.

She flicked her gaze to Joseph. He stood barely out of sight and waved his staff over a symbol on the floor. Quickly, she dragged her focus away and settled it on the vampire again. "It's obvious who wears the trousers in your relationship."

Lorenzo took a few steps back and blurred as he raced into the barrier. The sound was like a huge echoing crash and one of the panes in the glass door cracked. He smiled. "I'll tear you apart." That wasn't his voice—did that mean he and his creepy passenger shared control or was there inner conflict between them?

A little puzzled, she wondered why Joseph's work didn't seem to have any effect on the invader. Then, out of the corner of her eye, she saw the dead man with the gash in his neck rise to a seated position.

Lorenzo touched the shield softly, clearly testing it. He looked at Scott. "This is your work? You're good but it won't save you." He smiled menacingly at the young man and his fangs descended slowly.

While he spoke to her friend, she flicked a glance at the dead man. His eyes were milky white like the zombies she had seen in Palm Springs, but they'd had…personality. This one looked somehow empty and hungry. It jerked its head toward Lorenzo, who now walked backward to take another run at the shield.

The vampire hadn't noticed the dead man's action. He stopped inches from the undead's face, which jerked again in the direction of his hand.

It was covered in blood and she wondered whose but decided if Lorenzo had killed Dick, he'd have mentioned it by now.

The vampire sneered. "Even a magical shield can only take so many—"

Even through the closed door, the crunch of teeth on his hand was audible, followed by his pained howl.

He ripped his hand away and held it up. It was missing a finger but sadly, not the one the ring was on. He turned to the undead man and decapitated him with a blurring swing of his arm. A roar of pain followed and he cradled his hand. "Joseph, you're next."

Scott winced. "Did he hit that guy with the same hand?"

"He did," Lexi confirmed, knowing Lorenzo would be able to hear them without difficulty.

"He didn't think that through, did he?" Her friend smirked.

The vampire was clearly in agony and stared at his hand. In the place where he had been bitten, the skin began to turn black. Horror crept over his face as he looked at it, then at them, and suddenly vanished. Tiles slid to the ground from the low roof, the only evidence of his hasty retreat.

She spun to face Joseph. "What did you do?"

The man leaned heavily against the wall behind him. "I raised what was once my good friend to a zombie state. His bite was death."

His knees began to give way. She bolted toward him and caught him around the waist. Scott took his other side and his staff. They led him to a chair and lowered him gently. As his head drooped, the two friends shared a worried glance. Scott wrapped the man's arm around his staff and settled it against him.

Joseph looked at him and patted his hand.

Lexi pulled a chair up and sat beside him. "I'm sorry Lorenzo killed your friend…again."

The man nodded. "I would have drawn the spirit from him anyway to allow him true rest."

A dozen vampires landed in the courtyard and began to fling themselves repeatedly at the shield. It obviously hurt them, but their clan leader had told them to do it so they persisted. The cracked pane of glass shattered and others began to vibrate.

"The shield won't hold for much long—" Scott cut off as a glowing ball hovered over the courtyard. The vampires looked at it but didn't stop their assault.

The light from the ball grew in intensity, then blazed like the sun. The attackers covered their heads and curled on the ground, their screams of agony shrill and disquieting. The sorcerer looked away when they burst into flames.

The ball turned black and fell.

"What the hell was that? I've never seen anything like it."

"Is it safe to go out there now?" one of the shifters asked.

Joseph touched his head gingerly. "Let's give it a few minutes."

Scott looked at the man's wound. "Would you be offended if I treated that cut on your head?"

"I would be grateful." He smiled at him.

He took a bottle of water and cloth from his bag and set to work on the injury.

"Do you think it's over, then?" Lexi asked.

Joseph shook his head. "It's almost over for Lorenzo. His body will decay but you'll have to get to him quickly. His bite is contagious now. He could start an epidemic." He looked at her, his expression grim. "And you saw how strong Delphine is. She'll look for a new host."

She wiped her forehead. "Damn. There's no way to know where she'll go next."

The man winced as Scott dabbed at the cut. "She has a lust for blood. I think she'll choose another vampire."

The sorcerer sighed. "But how can we know which one before she kills again."

Lexi poked his arm. "He was right there. Why didn't you simply obliterate him?"

"I'd have had to bring down the shield to do it. I don't think I could have matched his speed."

The magical barrier hummed and she spun reflexively. Dick knocked a rat-tat-tat-tat on the shield. She sagged with relief, then gave him her angry face. "Where the hell have you been?"

"Lorenzo attacked Oberon's place before he came here."

Scott turned and moved to bring the shield down. As he did so, the vampire caught a glimpse of Joseph and concern flooded his face. He entered and hurried to the man.

"I'll be okay, old friend. I am merely tired."

Lexi looked out to see that Joseph's people and the shifters had begun to move the bodies into a storeroom on the other side of the courtyard.

Joseph interrupted, "Is Oberon—"

"He's fine. His friend Martine didn't fare so well. I managed to catch one of the witches and begged her to help me before she fled town. She gave me a couple of those fun balls. I could use a few more but I think all the witches have gone now."

"Perhaps they're the only ones with any sense," Lexi muttered.

Scott rubbed his face. "This is insane. Kindred has to intervene. He's killed what? Fifteen humans? That wasn't part of his deal."

Dick picked up a chair that had been toppled. "I would imagine the plan was to remove him anyway. He's a loose end and it fits the narrative. A supe goes crazy and Kindred steps in and deals with it. Everyone's happy. It makes me wonder how often this happens. This is turning into a perfect shit-storm."

"Could we go back to plan A and pull him out into the sun?" Lexi located a trashcan and held it out for the cloth and cotton wool Scott was discarding. "I feel less inclined to keep his clan alive."

The sorcerer shook his head. "Joseph won't be of any assistance for some time, I'm afraid."

She looked at the man. Her friend was right. Although the cut was healing, Joseph looked like he was probably magically spent. She peered into the courtyard at the piles of dust.

"Okay. We'll have to go after him. We'll try to get Delphine before she finds another host." She turned to Dick. "It's almost daylight. Can you get to the apartment and make sure Broullard's okay before you turn in?"

He fixed her with a disbelieving stare. "What's the plan? Is there a plan? Or will you simply run in there to kill Lorenzo with your sword out and your fingers crossed?"

"I won't target Lorenzo. I intend to kill the rest of his clan so Delphine will have nowhere to go. Then, we can wait for Lorenzo to die. Joseph, he won't turn into a vampire zombie, will he?"

"No. As he is overcome by the bite, he will simply decay."

Scott put his first-aid kit away. "Aren't you forgetting that she'll still have one place left to go? Into you."

"And that's assuming you don't get savaged by a roomful of vampires," Dick added.

Lexi looked at the two of them. "There can't be that many of them left. I'll go in like before. Invisible. It'll be fine."

The vampire looked doubtful. "They didn't know what was going on before. Even if you're invisible, it won't be so easy again."

"Fine. Do we have any other ideas?" She looked around the room.

"I have something that might help." Joseph put his hand into his pocket and withdrew a woman's ring.

She frowned at it. "That looks familiar."

"It sat for several years in a display case next to the one on Lorenzo's finger."

Lexi raised her eyebrows. "Marie Laveau's ring."

He nodded. "She won't possess you, but if she deems you worthy, she may assist you."

Without hesitation, she took the ring and slipped it onto her finger. She stared at the stone and waited to see if she felt different. Noticing the room was quiet, she glanced up. Every pair of eyes was on her. "What are you looking at? Get to work."

A collective sigh of relief filled the air.

Dick patted Joseph on the shoulder. "Right, well. I'll be off then." He walked to the door and turned to her. "Good luck, and don't get killed."

"I'll do my—" she started.

The door closed and he was gone.

"Best."

CHAPTER TWENTY-FIVE

Lexi stood in the alley a few doors down from Lorenzo's bar. She looked across to the alley on the opposite side of the street where her friend stood with a handful of shifters.

Anxious to make as little noise as possible, she mouthed, "Is he there?"

He shrugged and couldn't hear her, obviously. She peeked out along the street and studied their target.

"What was that?"

She jumped and spun defensively. Scott was directly behind her. "I have a sword in my hand, you dimwit."

"Sorry. I couldn't hear you."

Her sigh revealed her irritation. "I asked if Lorenzo's in there."

"Yes, he's there. George has had someone watching the place. He turned up a few minutes before sunrise."

Satisfied, she returned her focus to the building they were watching. "That was cutting it close. Can you pinpoint where he is in there?"

The sorcerer closed his eyes. "The ring is on the second floor now. So unless he's already passed it on to someone else, he's up there too."

Lexi turned to him. "Do you think that's possible?

"Possible yes, likely…no."

"Okay. I'll go in. Give me sixty seconds, then you come in with the shifters."

He scowled. "I should go in there with you."

"You need to protect the shifters. I can shield the sound of my heartbeat but not a roomful of shifters. If that building is full of vampires, I don't want to be responsible for Agatha losing her father. And we'll be in there sixty seconds apart. I'll barely have time to use the magic before you're there again."

Scott took her hand and attempted to transfer more magic to her.

"You won't get any more into me. The tank's full, but I'll be using it fast when I go invisible, so stay close but safe inside that building."

He nodded and vanished. She looked across the road to where he stood with the shifters once more. As she put her hand on the scar, about to make herself invisible, a car roared past the alley and screeched to a halt.

She looked across at the others with a shrug she hoped asked the burning question in her mind. *What's going on?*

The sorcerer appeared next to her again. "Some idiot in a sports car parked outside the bar."

Lexi looked at George and the other shifters who seemed to have lost all sense and forgotten they were supposed to be hiding. They crowded out in front of the alley and looked at Lorenzo's bar with their jaws dropped.

"Yoo-hoo!"

Lexi's eyes widened at the sound of Dick's voice. "What's that fucking vampire up to now?" She stuck her head out and scowled. He stood in front of the bar and waved at the security camera. She pointed in his direction. "I want to know what he's saying. Now!"

CHAPTER TWENTY-SIX

Lorenzo had burst through the door of his bar with his hand wrapped in cloth. He'd avoided the gazes of his few remaining clan members as he walked through to the stairs leading to the second floor. "I'm going upstairs. I don't want to be disturbed."

Darnell had taken two steps and stopped. "Where are the others?"

He stopped, turned, and opened his mouth to speak but found himself staring speculatively at each face. After a few moments, he became aware that it wasn't he who looked at them. It was her. She was looking for her next host. He spun away and climbed the stairs.

Now, he paced the room, his mind in a fog. How could this have gone so fucking badly?

Perhaps you need blood. Delphine purring in his mind was the last thing he needed.

A huge part of him wanted to rip the ring from his hand, but he couldn't bring himself to do it. Instead, he unwound the cloth from it and stared in horror. The whole hand was black.

"I'll have to lose my hand. It's not the end of the world." He pulled his jacket off and froze at the sight of black veins climbing his arm and disappearing into his shirt sleeve. He raced into the bathroom to a mirror and yanked his shirt off. The buttons pinged in different directions but his gaze was glued to the black veins which extended beyond his shoulder and onto his chest. It was too late. "Fuck! Fuck, fuck, fuck."

Lorenzo looked at the expression of disgust on his face in the mirror. It was her again.

He punched it and glass fell into the sink below.

A sound behind him drew his attention. He looked around the door. Five of his clan had gathered in his living room. "I said I didn't want to be disturbed. What do you want?"

"I thought—" Darnell stopped speaking. He seemed confused but his gaze wasn't on his boss' face. It was on his black hand.

"Thought what?" He moved his hand behind his back.

The man shook his head in apparent confusion. "You called us. Didn't you call us?"

It wasn't the hand they were looking at, he realized. It was the ring calling to them the same way it had seduced him.

"Get out," Lorenzo shouted. Automatically, his hand came from behind to shoo them away.

They didn't move, however, and stared fixedly at the ring for a long moment before they began to edge forward. He'd had enough. Fury surged and he moved through the room faster than they could track him. When he returned to his previous position, the bodies lay on his carpet and began to desiccate.

"Is there anyone else you'd like to call out to, bitch?" he bellowed into the empty room.

The doorbell sounded and he heard someone shout, "Yoo-hoo!"

His teeth gritted in frustration, he moved to the desk and looked at the security screen. He flicked a couple of buttons until he looked through the camera at the front entrance and gaped at the screen as he tried to comprehend what he saw.

William Levine—or Dick as the idiot called himself these days—stood outside in the street during the day and leaned on a gallery post in front of his building. He didn't stand in direct sunlight but it was daytime, and this wasn't normal. On the screen, he could see the light creeping slowly down the post. He stared in fascination as it moved inexorably toward his visitor's head.

He checked the time, then looked at the screen again. At that point, he realized Dick made no effort to even cover his eyes. How could he stand it?

Agonizingly slow seconds ticked past until the sun met the vampire's hair and began to slide slowly over his face. He scrolled through a cellphone screen, seemingly oblivious to the process.

Lorenzo was transfixed and unable to drag his gaze away. He stared until Dick's face was fully bathed in light. Finally—lazily—the vampire retrieved a pair of sunglasses from his pocket and slid them on.

As frozen and shocked as her host was, Delphine was quite the opposite. She raved and screamed inside him. Her spirit threw itself at Dick in a tsunami of wanton desire. The vampire outside seemed completely oblivious to her attentions, but Lorenzo could barely hear himself think.

He finally spun away from the screen. Their visitor spoke again and she twisted him to gaze at the screen.

"This is some kind of trick. The feed's not live. It's a recording." He pressed a button and a disc ejected from the equipment, but Dick was still there. His voice was audible and he smiled cheerfully. "Good morning. It's a beautiful day." He exchanged pleasantries with people on the street below.

I want him, Delphine moaned.

No.

"What do you care? You'll be dead in a few hours. Don't you want vengeance?"

"How is this vengeance?" he asked aloud.

I'll wear him like little Amy. I'll walk him to his friends and tear them to pieces. For you. I'll do it for you.

He dropped into a chair and sat with his face in his hands, feeling wretched. After a moment, he pulled his hand away quickly. It smelled of decay.

While Dick had apparently been too far away to feel the pull of Delphine's spirit, the clan had not. The remaining ten of them had shuffled up the stairs, filed into the room, and stared at him with hunger in their eyes. Lorenzo roared and dispatched them all—his own clan. He honestly didn't care. If he wouldn't live, neither would they. He finished and swayed dizzily.

Why did you do that? She sounded suspicious.

"I've made my decision. I want revenge. Did you want *him* as your next host or one of them? I merely removed his competition." He didn't care whether she believed him or not.

But you're weak now. One of them could have bested him.

Don't worry, Delphine. I have one last fight in me.

Perhaps revenge was all that was left. But it wouldn't be the revenge she wanted. While there was still strength in him, he'd destroy this sun-walking William Levine. He'd hold the vampire's heart in his hand and let her watch through his eyes as he crushed it.

He turned to the security equipment and reached for the microphone.

CHAPTER TWENTY-SEVEN

Lexi stood with Scott in the alley, out of sight of Lorenzo's bar. Whatever stupid gambit Dick was up to, she didn't want to get him killed any faster than he was already likely to be. She watched as he stood at the door in full view of the camera and scrolled through his cellphone. Periodically, he swiped left or right with a nonchalant motion. "What the hell is he doing?"

Her companion glimpsed out. "I think he's on Tinder."

"Get him on the phone. We had a perfectly workable plan." She was furious.

Scott dialed Dick's cell and they waited while he picked invisible fluff from his jacket sleeve and ELO's "Mister Blue Sky" began to play. Finally, he held the cellphone up, rejected the call, and dropped it into his pocket. Her face fell into a grim expression. "I'll break his neck again." She could see the vampire roll his eyes so he'd clearly heard her.

The security system hissed into life. "Hello, Dick."

"Loren—no, wait. It's Delphine, isn't it?" He sounded thoroughly enchanted. "How are you, my dear? I understand I just missed you at Joseph's place. I'm simply devastated. We must catch up."

Lorenzo's voice sounded almost coquettish. "Let me see when I can…fit you in."

He grinned. "Ooh! You minx. I'm free now. How about break-fast at Brennan's? They do a wonderful dish—Eggs Hussarde, with the most divine Marchand De Vin sauce. They also have a cocktail called a Corpse Reviver. I'm sure Lorenzo might be interested in trying it. How's his hand?" Dick finally glanced in Lexi's direction with a raised eyebrow as the other vampire attempted to regain control of his vocal cords, which resulted in a strangled growl. "Delphine darling, is that your stomach growling? I'll tell you what. Since I'm here, why don't I pop in now? We can order in."

The door buzzed and he disappeared inside.

Scott turned to Lexi. "Well, now what?"

"Fuck! Get the others. We're going in." She wasn't sure who she wanted to kill first out of Lorenzo and Dick.

The sorcerer appeared across the road where he spoke to the shifters, and she stroked the scar and thought the word "hidden." Dick had shoved a piece of paper in the door on his way in to stop it from closing properly. She ran into the bar with her katana drawn and whirled in all directions, expecting an attack, but was met with silence. When she saw no other vampires, she dropped the invisibility to conserve her magic and hurried through to the back of the bar. She forced herself to move slowly and quietly as she crept up the stairs.

Lorenzo's apartment was directly in front of her. Dick stood in the doorway and the other vampire was in the room, facing them. A playful smile played on his lips but in a moment, it was gone. Lexi registered the shift from Delphine to her host. She pushed a shield around Dick as their adversary blurred toward him. The attacking vampire bounced off it but was on his feet again in an instant.

Lexi tried to push a shield around Dick again, but her magic was depleted.

There was no time to plan but Lorenzo didn't target him anyway. The ring was on her hand before she could react.

Delphine's voice began to speak to her. *Go to the daywalker. Put the ring on the day walker's hand. Why are you not moving? Do what you're told. I order you.*

She ignored it because honestly, she didn't feel controlled by the spirit. At the same time, she felt something was different.

"Lexi." Dick spoke in urgent tones. "Take it off—quickly." He approached her and tried to catch her hand, but she pushed him away. He catapulted across the room and onto his back in the blink of an eye. She looked at her hand in surprise as she hadn't meant to do that.

That's it. While he's on the floor, put the ring on him.

Delphine's voice didn't sound remotely seductive. It was whiny.

Lexi strode to Lorenzo. He sprawled on the floor and looked defeated. She caught him by the throat and lifted him. It felt remarkable like this was the kind of strength she was always meant to have. This was her birthright.

She gazed into his eyes. He looked terrified and she liked that. "What did I tell you? I said he's off-limits. Do you not remember me saying that?" She looked at his arm where it hung black and useless at his side. She grasped one of his decaying fingers and twisted. It came away easily and she dropped it as he screamed.

That's right. Give him pain.

"Stop screaming." She shook him. "I need to ask you something."

He silenced himself. She stared at him and realized that he was little more than a wreck of a man.

"Are you listening?" She felt the muscles in his neck work, which she assumed was him trying to nod.

He looked into her eyes, then away, and clearly didn't like what he saw there.

"Does she talk like this all the time?" She loosened her grip slightly to allow him to answer.

Lorenzo sniveled and choked out a, "Yes. It never stops, even when I'm trying to sleep."

She shook her head. "How annoying."

"And the compulsion to do what she says," he continued. "It's relentless."

"Compulsion?" Lexi thought for a moment and listened to Delphine's ceaseless speech. "I don't get that. Only the irritating chatter."

Dick touched her shoulder. She turned to look at him and he stepped back with shock on his face. "Lexi, your eyes."

In that moment, she knew her eyes were black, but she couldn't say how she knew.

She drew her arm up to backhand him. But while her attention was diverted, Lorenzo ripped the ring from her finger and threw it across the room.

Lexi turned slowly to look at him. The expression on his face gave her pause. She tilted her head as though a different angle might give her a new perspective on this cockroach in her hand. Finally, she decided he looked confused. "Not what you expected?" she asked, conversationally. "But thank you. She was annoying."

Before he could answer, she snapped his neck with a twist of her wrist and let him fall.

Her eyes were still black. She looked at the scar and noticed that it was filled with what looked like shiny, wet, black tar.

Scott entered the room, paused, and stared at her in horror. She shook her head before her eyes became soft, brown, and desperate.

A voice that wasn't her own or Delphine's spoke from her mouth. "She needs your magic, boy. I can't hold her except for a few seconds."

He raced to her, grasped both her arms, and began to push his magic through the blood bond and into her.

Her eyes went black again and she snarled and fought. He tried to take her power away and she knew she had the power to strike him and kill him, but something stopped her.

"I'll kill you," Lexi screamed.

The young sorcerer gritted his teeth and hung on.

Dick scrambled to his feet behind her, wound his arms around her, and pinned the tops of her arms to her sides.

Scott looked frantically from one hand to the other. "Where's the ring?"

"It's over there on the floor." The vampire gestured with his head.

The other man's eyes widened. "How can the ring do this from over there?"

A hand settled on her head and she twisted to see that Anne had arrived with James and Sam.

The witch removed her hand abruptly. "This isn't the ring. It's something else."

"Help us, please," Scott cried.

They encircled Lexi, Scott, and Dick.

Anne began to chant. "Banish the negative harm and pain, only positive shall remain."

James and Sam took up the chant. A breeze lifted around them and grew in intensity until finally, the black-painted windows in Lorenzo's apartment exploded and the wind howled away.

Lexi felt the strength leave her body. She slumped, almost unconscious. As if from a distance, she watched as her scar filled with white energy before her eyes closed.

When she woke again, she knew they were back to normal but something was different. She looked around the room. Scott's bed was empty and she was still in her clothes.

Whispered snatches of conversation drifted to her. "But she didn't even have the ring on at that point."

Lexi felt wiped out. She sat, gave it a few seconds, then stood and walked up the hallway.

When she rounded the corner into the room, Dick held Marcel up and waved his little paw at her. "Anne's asking about the day-walking thing." He turned to the woman. "Lexi knows. She was there in Chicago when a witch threw a spell pouch that exploded all over me. I spent a night paralyzed and now, I can walk in the daylight."

Joseph nodded. "I can confirm that every word he speaks is truth."

She almost snorted at the Joseph-stamp-of-approval. Every word *was* true, but Dick had woven together three barely connected incidents. She glanced around. No one seemed inclined to call him a liar and she wouldn't say anything. If it ever got back to Kindred that Scott had done this for him, he'd be sentenced to death—or, at the very least, life in The Hollows.

Anne shuffled to the edge of her seat. "What was in the pouch?"

Lexi was surprised she hadn't taken a notepad and pen out.

The vampire opened his arms, his palms up, in an exaggerated shrug. "I have no idea. I wasn't able to get the muck out of the fabric. By the time I knew I'd be able to sunbathe in the South of France again, the suit had been discarded."

The woman sat back muttering, "I wonder what it was."

It was Geraldine's turn to lean forward. "So you didn't need to crawl into my father's tomb."

Dick winced. "Ah! No, I'm afraid not."

"Well, I hope that ruined another suit. You deserve it." She scowled at him.

The vampire put his hand over hers. "I apologize unreservedly."

Geraldine looked at his hand, then at him with an eyebrow raised. "And making poor Betsy climb in there with you. You're a very bad man."

Scott passed a cup of coffee to Lexi. She glanced quickly at him but had to look away. The desire she had felt to kill him was still fresh in her mind and she felt ashamed. The worst thing was that he would have felt her feelings through the blood bond—the murder and the shame. She focused instead on Geraldine. "You're looking well."

The shifter smiled at Scott. "Well, your man here is quite the physician. It's not a cure but I think he might have given me another year or two."

Anne stood and looked down at her. "I might have a few things to give you another year on top of that. Visit me at the shop."

Geraldine stood. "I'll walk out with you."

The two women said their goodbyes and left.

Lexi removed Marie Laveau's ring and handed it to Joseph. "Did you get the other ring?"

"Yes. I will put the spirit within it to rest."

She turned to Broullard. "Detective—"

"I think you can call me Charles." He smiled.

"You never mentioned that Alice is a police officer. Why not?"

"Ah! Well, the simple answer is that she kind of is and kind of isn't a police officer."

"That's the simple answer?" She frowned at him.

"She used to be a uniform but was posted to what most officers call the Special Ops team."

Lexi was familiar with the process of Kindred legacies joining the police force to work on supernatural cases, keeping the details off the official books.

He cleared his throat and looked uncomfortable. "Whatever

you say she is, I've known her for years—not well but well enough. I felt protective of her and feared you meant to harm her. We look after our own."

She sighed. "I don't mean her any harm. What would be the point?"

Peter walked in from Dick's apartment. "The popcorn's popped and the movie's ready to go."

"Excellent." The vampire picked Marcel up and turned to the detective. "Charles, would you like to come and see one of my movies?"

"I'd love to, thank you." Broullard said good evening and followed them to the door.

"It's Peter's favorite," Dick explained. "*A Long Dark Night in Hollywood.*"

As the door closed, Lexi heard Broullard ask, "Don't you die at the end of that one?"

Joseph looked at Lexi. "Did you find your answers in the end?"

She shrugged. "I found a problem I thought I'd already solved and answers to questions I never asked. Does that count?"

He sighed. "Ah yes, your friend Caleb. What will you do about that?"

Her brain flooded with the questions and concerns she'd stored away while dealing with Lorenzo. "I don't know. It's clear now, though, that he knew we would be looking for him. He created that doppelganger out of a living person merely to make them a target so they'd die instead of him. I'm not happy about that."

"So, you simply forget him?" the man asked,

Scott answered from the kitchen. "How can we do that? He's trying to bring that demon across into our realm. If we don't do something, it'll be mayhem. But if we pursue him, we'll take on the whole of Kindred. There are only four of us."

Joseph stood and picked his staff up. "I think you'll find, when the time comes, that there will be many more than four of you."

Lexi met his eyes. "I hope so."

He patted her on the shoulder. "Before you go, you should take a ride on the *Creole Queen* paddlewheel boat. Try the gumbo and listen to a jazz band play on the Mississippi."

"Maybe we'll do that." She frowned when she realized he had taken Delphine's ring out and held it in his hand. "Will it be complicated? Drawing the spirit out?"

"No. I have everything I need. I could do it here. Scott, would you like to help?"

"Sure." The young sorcerer was always excited by new magic.

"Can you clear a space over there?" Joseph pulled a pouch from his pocket.

Scott moved a table to the side of the room and the other man told him to cup his hands. "We need a circle—big enough for the ring, is all."

The young man watched the particles pour into his hand from the pouch. "What is that? Sand?"

"It's cornmeal."

He allowed the cornmeal to pour slowly out of his hand in the vague shape of a circle but didn't look happy with the result. "It's not a very good circle. Would you like me to do it again?"

Joseph chuckled. "No, it will suffice." He passed the ring to Scott, who placed it inside the circle and sat on the floor beside it, not wanting to miss a thing.

The other man chanted and twisted his staff so the bones on strings clattered against it. The sorcerer's gaze on the ring was almost hypnotic and his face moved closer until his nose was barely outside the circle.

The chanting ceased and there was silence for two seconds before the staff pounded onto the ring and shattered it.

Scott's entire body left the floor as he hurtled away. "Jesus!"

Joseph chuckled. "The ring merely needed to be destroyed."

"So, what was all the ritual stuff for?" The sorcerer had his hand over his chest.

The old man beamed. "Fun."

Lexi exhaled a sharp breath. "Well, I could have destroyed it."

The old voodoo priest's eyes glittered. "Where's the fun in that?"

She grinned as Scott scraped the metal and stone up.

"Joseph, you are a funny, funny man." He held the pieces of the ring out, but the other man was nowhere to be seen.

He shrugged, stood, and threw the pieces of jewelry into the trash before he headed to the door.

Lexi folded her arms. "Where are you going?"

"To watch the movie." He pointed at the door.

"And the cornmeal you sprinkled all over the floor will clean itself up, will it?"

Scott looked at the mess and then at her. "Yes." He clicked his fingers and it was gone.

"Smartass."

EPILOGUE

"So you won't do anything about the doppelgänger?" Dick's eyebrow was raised in surprise.

"What's the point? It's not like she's stolen my life. She's wearing my face, yes, but that wasn't her doing—or, most likely, the person she was before. Why even tell her what she is? She has her life and I have mine. I think it's best if I simply leave. We still have Caleb to deal with." Lexi, Scott, and Dick looked out from the deck of the Creole Queen. A long drive awaited them but for now, she felt they deserved a few hours R and R.

The paddle began to turn, the jazz band struck up, and the boat glided through the water.

A handful of people stood on the shore and waved but mostly, they continued with their day.

Scott turned to Dick. "What about you? Do you regret day-walking now? It's all anyone's talking about."

He raised a finger in the air. "But they're all talking about a witch and a spell pouch. You're off the hook. I think it's worked out rather well."

Lexi turned and leaned her back against the rail. "I wonder if things will settle here now that New Orleans is two vampire clans lighter."

The vampire raised an eyebrow. "Pfft! Almost half of the Quarter is up for grabs. I think it's a good time to get out of town." He pointed along the boat. "Unless I'm very much mistaken, I think the bar's this way." He wandered in that direction.

She turned to look at the shore again.

Scott did the same. "When is Dolores expecting us in Charlotte?"

"Not for another—" She froze as she found herself looking into what seemed to be her own eyes. It was Alice. Her hair was the same color and her build identical. The only differences were the angry scars raked across her face. The doppelgänger stared at her with wide, horror-filled eyes.

Scott spun quickly. "I'll speak to her." He materialized beside the woman and opened his mouth to speak.

The next moments for Lexi were like watching herself but it all happened much faster.

Before her friend seemed to have managed a single word, Alice acted defensively. She swept her hand across her thigh, exactly where Lexi's dimensional pocket was located. A glint in her hand preceded a swipe. The woman looked quickly at her before she raced away and left Scott alone. His mouth shaped into an O and his eyes were wide as a bloom of red appeared on the chest of his white t-shirt. He stumbled and his gaze sought hers as he fell. She opened her mouth to scream but nothing emerged.

Pain and fear surged through the empathetic link and she looked around. The boat, the shore, and the distance all seemed impossible.

I have to be there.

In the next moment, she was. She wobbled to her knees and vomited. Lexi stumbled to her feet a few feet away from him, his agony intense through the empathetic link of their blood bond.

Lexi dropped to her knees and tears streamed down her face as bubbles of blood came from his mouth. A hand caught hers and she looked at Dick, who had appeared beside her. He was soaking wet from the waist down. She realized he wasn't holding her hand. Instead, he held her arm out, his expression compelling. She looked at the scar and recognized the presence of the white magic. She still had magic? Shit!

Quickly, she put her hand over her friend's chest. Sensing the hole in his heart, she poured out her desire for it to be healed.

The vampire eased her back by her shoulders. "His heart's beating. I think he'll be okay."

She stood and glowered in the direction in which Alice had disappeared. "Make sure I don't lose him," she told Dick coldly.

"How am I supposed to—"

"You know what I'm saying. I will not lose him."

He nodded once and prepared to bite into his own wrist.

Lexi ran after the doppelgänger. She'd intended to leave her alone but now, she would crush her. Fury fueled her pace but the area was deserted. She couldn't know if her quarry had continued in the same direction or turned off so she chose the direction that made the most sense to her.

As she ran past a building near the tracks, the woman lurched out with a knife in her hand. She had half-expected it as it was what she'd have done. Unfortunately, that was where the similarities ended. She mostly managed to dodge the knife, but it sliced her arm before she kicked it from the assailant's hand. The girl swept a hand across her vest and another one appeared. Lexi did the same.

Her adversary blurred as she moved quickly to attack again. The speed was shocking. It was like fighting a vampire except they always tried to bite when they fought and were predictable. Alice wasn't. Without warning, she flicked the blade at her. She ducked her head and felt the sharp sting along the edge of her ear. The woman had cut her twice now.

Alice didn't retrieve another blade but somehow looked more dangerous, crouched as she was like a shifter about to turn. She flicked a shuriken and it bit into Lexi's shoulder as she twisted to avoid it. Before she could regain her balance, her opponent picked her up and hurled her through a window in the side of the building. She landed in what looked like an abandoned workshop.

The woman stood outside and glared at her where she lay dazed. "Why would anyone make such a weak doppelgänger of me? What's the point?" She vaulted through the window but stopped and shook her head as though dizzy, then continued toward Lexi and dragged her onto her knees by the hair. The familiar sound of the button being pulled from the vest indicated the release of the garroting wire. She tensed, then froze as she heard the unmistakable squeal as the wire coiled in again. Alice had released it and stumbled into the back of her.

"What have you…done to me?" She sounded suddenly exhausted, which made no sense at all. She hadn't done anything to the girl…yet.

Lexi felt suddenly powerful. "Scott only wanted to talk to you, Alice. You almost killed him."

"It's Alicia."

Acting on pure adrenaline, she grabbed the woman and flung her the length of the room. She bulldozed into a row of cupboard doors and splintered them.

Alicia scrambled behind a row of desks, her breathing labored.

Lexi drew her katana and scraped it along the worktops as she walked along chanting, "Alicia, Alicia, not gonna miss ya."

Where did that come from?

"What?"

Lexi leapt over the desk and swung her fist into the woman's head to leave her dazed. She elbowed her in the face and was amazed to see her slide across the floor and impact the wall behind with extreme force. Driven by cold anger, she grasped the girl by the vest and punched her repeatedly in the face. The more she did it, the stronger she felt. She was starting to enjoy this and hadn't felt this strong since— A vision of herself holding Lorenzo by the throat came to her. She stopped, let go of Alicia's vest, and grimaced when the girl fell.

Breathing hard, she drew herself tall and looked at the doppelgänger. The face so eerily her own was slick with blood.

How many times did I hit her?

As she dropped to her knees, she drew the katana from her pocket. It was time to simply finish this and get the job done. "I intended to simply leave town. You brought this on yourself." She wasn't even sure the girl was conscious as she spoke to her.

With the blade held above her head, she felt power pulse through her.

She was ready to strike when the door flew open.

"Lexi, stop. She's not a doppelgänger. She's your sister."

Something in the tone penetrated and she froze and stared at the bloody girl with her face. She put the sword down and looked at Scott. He wasn't alone. Dick was there and so was someone else. She looked into the face of the man beside Scott.

He was older. Of course he was—he'd been fifteen when she'd last seen him. Before she'd been made to forget him, made to forget he'd been bitten by a shifter, made to forget being dragged out of the room, and made to forget she'd heard the shot.

"Bryan?"

Being distracted, Lexi didn't see the powerful right hook from the girl on the floor.

The lights went out.

The story continues with book three, THE RISING LEGACY, coming soon to Amazon and Kindle Unlimited.

There are many great things about writing for a career. Making characters come to life on the page is probably the top one. Having people I've never met fall in love with those characters is a firm number two. Now, not everyone will agree with my number three, but it has got to be research. I'll be honest... not ALL research. Not the days I spent researching the history of sporks for another series I wrote; jeez I'll never get those days back. But the research I did for The Bound Legacy involved flying to New Orleans. It was one of the best vacatio... research trips I've ever had.

I knew I wanted it to be the setting of book 2 but I still didn't have a clue what Lexi's case was going to be. So, I spent the time strolling through the French Quarter with my husban... research assistant, Phil. We researched the hell out of those bars, studied beignets inside and out, became intimately acquainted with po'boys, and just in case. We researched everywhere a scene of The Originals had been filmed. You know, just to be thorough.

It was on a Vampires, Ghosts & Voodoo tour that I finally had my *aha!* moment. I had my plot. And a tour of The Museum of Death (not recommended for the faint-of-heart) gave me my first scene. I had to walk around that place alone because my husband wouldn't go inside. When I came out, he proudly told me he'd been hit on by a transexual sex worker. Apparently, I was lucky he was still there waiting for me because according to him, he's clearly still got the moves. Phil himself was a valuable source of inspiration. One of the scenes wouldn't have been written if he hadn't been tricked by a couple of conmen on Decatur Street.

"Don't worry dear, I'll kill that guy in the book." – And I did.

Roll on a few months and life had thrown more than my fair share of curve-balls at me. I was still working on the book with a brain so mangled with everything that was going on, I needed help. Luckily, I found myself in the right place. Where? Vegas of course. The 20Booksto50k conference provided me with knowledge and inspiration. Also, there may have been karaoke and a zipline. Without the wonderful advice of Michael, the hours of support from Charles Tillman, Erika Everest and the Ladies of LMBPN, I don't think I'd have made it past the post.

But, here we are. I hope you enjoy this installment of Legacy of the Shadow's Blood.

Elaine

Sign up for E.G. Bateman's email list and receive your free copy of *The Fugitive Legacy*, the exciting prequel to the Legacy of the Shadow's Blood series.

With faulty powers and a vampire attack, can Lexi do what's right?

Lexi has worked extra hard to compensate for her faulty paranormal abilities and prove she deserves her place among the supernatural protectors, Kindred.

The aftermath of a vampire attack leaves her questioning her loyalties.

Can she hide her secret? Or will she be forced to flee from the only family she has ever known?

But Kindred don't just let you leave...

<u>Get your free copy here.</u>

https://www.bookbub.com/authors/michael-anderle